'Arun?'

His name escaped in a sigh so soft Arun was sure she hadn't meant to say it, but he responded anyway, bending over her again to brush the honey-tasting lips with his. To brush her name, 'Melissa', on them.

The chemistry that had worked between them from their first meeting flared back to life. Arun's hand slid around the back of her head, his fingers weaving into her hair, holding her captive.

The kiss deepened. Arun felt the power of it as desire shuddered through his body, tightening his muscles and heating his blood.

This was madness.

The baby—

They should stop—

She broke away from the kiss—but not before he'd felt enough of her response to know the chemistry still worked for her as well.

DESERT DOCTORS

Two sheikh brothers claim their brides

Twin brothers Kamid and Arun Rahman al'Kawali, heirs to the throne of Zaheer, are using their exceptional medical skills to help their people. Devoted to duty, these proud and passionate princes of the desert are determined not to lose their hearts. But two strong yet vulnerable women are about to steal them away…

THE SHEIKH SURGEON'S BABY

BY
MEREDITH WEBBER

MILLS & BOON®
Pure reading pleasure™

All the characters in this book have no existence outside
the imagination of the author, and have no relation
whatsoever to anyone bearing the same name or names.
They are not even distantly inspired by any individual
known or unknown to the author, and all the incidents
are pure invention.

First published in Great Britain 2008
Large Print edition 2008
Harlequin Mills & Boon Limited,
Eton House, 18-24 Paradise Road,
Richmond, Surrey TW9 1SR

© Meredith Webber 2008

ISBN: 978 0 263 19988 8

Set in Times Roman 16½ on 19¼ pt.
17-1108-48223

Printed and bound in Great Britain
by Antony Rowe Ltd, Chippenham, Wiltshire

Meredith Webber says of herself, 'Some ten years ago, I read an article which suggested that Mills and Boon were looking for new medical authors. I had one of those "I can do that" moments, and gave it a try. What began as a challenge has become an obsession— though I do temper the "butt on seat" career of writing with dirty but healthy outdoor pursuits, fossicking through the Australian Outback in search of gold or opals. Having had some success in all of these endeavours, I now consider I've found the perfect lifestyle.'

Recent titles by the same author:

DESERT DOCTOR, SECRET SHEIKH**
A PREGNANT NURSE'S CHRISTMAS WISH
THE NURSE HE'S BEEN WAITING FOR*
HIS RUNAWAY NURSE
THE SPANISH DOCTOR'S CONVENIENT BRIDE

**Desert Doctors*
Crocodile Creek: 24-Hour Rescue

CHAPTER ONE

MELISSA peered out the window as the plane touched down. The late afternoon sun made mirrors of the sides of new, glass-fronted, high-rise towers so here and there square, earth coloured, flat-roofed dwellings were reflected in them, marrying old and new.

Zaheer! The country that had only been an exotic name to her was about to become a reality. Land of red desert sands and sweet oases, camels resting in the shade of stumpy date palms; land of desert warriors who'd once guarded travellers along the trade routes from west to east, some of their descendants still living a nomadic life.

'I would love to show you the desert,' Arun had said to her. They'd been lying in bed, watching the sun rise over the sea, knowing they were soon to part for ever, the magic they'd discovered together in the fortnight of the huge heart symposium in Hawaii already becoming a memory.

Now here she was, about to see the desert, though whether Arun would be the one showing it to her she didn't know. True, she'd be seeing him. After all, her best friend was about to marry his twin, but how would he treat her?

Politely, for sure—he was a very polite man.

Formally?

Probably, for this was his country and he had a certain position to uphold.

But the Arun she'd known had been a strong and generous lover, not a polite and formal sheikh.

The Arun she'd known…

She pressed her hand against the small bulge beneath the all-concealing caftan she was wearing. How he'd treat her wasn't really the issue—how he'd react was!

A feeling, so akin to panic her palms sweated, gripped her body.

She should have told him earlier.

But how, when she'd been so uncertain herself? When, even now, she was in a total muddle over the baby she was carrying. How ironic that she, the strong, efficient leader of a paediatric surgical team, a woman who could make split-second decisions that could mean life or death, should be reduced to a numb-brained blob of ectoplasm when she tried to sort out her thoughts about something as normal and natural as a pregnancy.

But she *should* have told him…

Arun stood inside the glass partition and watched the front door on the plane open, the stairs roll into place. In a couple of months the new airport would be operational and passengers would emerge into a tunnel, to be disgorged into the airport proper. But for now they had to clamber down the stairs.

He and Kam, his twin, on the rare occasions they'd returned from England for school holidays, had been met at the bottom of those stairs, the big cars lined up waiting for them to be whisked away to the family compound by their father's minions. Progress had stopped this practice but he *had* been allowed into the customs area the better to help the parents of the soon-to-be consort of the ruling sheikh, through the red tape of arrival in a foreign country.

All these thoughts flitted through his head as the stairs were secured. Were they a diversion—distracting him from thinking of the woman he was also meeting? The coincidence wasn't all that strange. After all, Melissa, hearing he was from Zaheer, had approached him at the heart symposium they'd both attended four months ago. She'd been eager to learn something of the country where her best friend was working.

He'd been struck first by her smile—by the way it had lit up her face—and the red-gold hair that had sprung with such vibrant life around her head. Then somehow the magic of attraction had worked between them, two people who hadn't wanted commitment drawn into a brief but heated and very satisfying affair.

That Melissa's best friend was now about to marry Arun's brother was the coincidence.

Or was it fate?

His desert ancestors may have believed their lives had been governed by the capricious whims of fate, but he, a modern man of science, refused to go along with it. Although it was certainly strange to think he'd be meeting Melissa again.

Strange and exciting, his body suggested. But continuing what they'd both agreed would begin and end at the symposium would surely be impossible. She was here for Jenny and Kam's wedding—her free time would be spent with her friend.

Or would it? Once he'd known she was coming, he had emailed her to ask if she'd mind doing some advisory work for him at the hospital. Perhaps fate did exist, he conceded. Just as he was about to set up a paediatric surgical ward at the hospital, an expert in paediatric surgery was arriving on his doorstep. Melissa would be able to tell him, from practical experience, what was needed in the way of equipment, how best the various services should be located, and what staffing levels he would require from the beginning.

Had he had an ulterior motive in asking this? Had he hoped she might prolong her stay? So they could renew their affair?

Surely not, when the non-hospital, non-work part of his mind should be focussed on the promise he'd made to Jenny and Kam—on finding a wife and beginning a family.

Melissa's reply had been brief and to the point—she would be happy to advise him. But she hadn't said how long she could remain in Zaheer, and he hadn't wanted to question Jenny about Melissa's plans in case he revealed their brief relationship had gone further than that of chance-met acquaintances.

The first passenger emerged from the plane, a woman, turning to speak to the older couple coming behind her. His body recognised her before his eyes did, stirring as it had stirred in heated dreams over the last four months.

The madly curling red-gold hair was covered

by a blue shawl, but bits were escaping, spring-ing with vibrant life around her face, and even from a distance he could see the wide smile that turned her regular, even unremarkable features into warm, irresistible beauty

Melissa!

He straightened his shoulders, tightened his gut, told his body to behave, and stepped forward, ready to greet the threesome as a bowing steward led them across the tarmac towards a private door into the customs area.

Excitement vied with apprehension as Mel came down the steps from the plane. Here she was, arriving in the country Arun had talked of with such deep passion she had smelt the dry desert air and seen images of oases, although they'd been in waterlocked Hawaii. Here she was, about to be reunited with her best friend, for the joyous occasion of Jenny's wedding.

Here she was, four months pregnant, and no one in the world other than herself knew…

Well, to be honest, her specialist knew…

She accompanied Jenny's parents across the tarmac, Jane Stapleton chattering, probably from nerves, about the first-class plane trip, the wonder of Jenny finally falling in love again—speculating about the man who'd healed her daughter's broken heart.

Mel could have told her something about the man—about his looks anyway—for Arun and Kam were identical twins. But the twins were obviously not identical in character, Kam about to commit to marriage, while Arun, by his own admission, had no intention of ever marrying again—or ever entering a long-term relationship.

'Two commitment-phobes,' Mel had teased when he'd told her this in Hawaii. 'The perfect match!'

How could a commitment-phobe commit to bringing up a baby? How would she, who knew nothing of motherhood, handle it? That was her biggest worry. Her constant worry!

One of many, to be honest. Childbirth was another, though she knew intellectually that was nonsense—something she had to get past—and how she'd juggle a baby and a job was a real concern.

Then there was the very real issue of single motherhood. Didn't a baby deserve two parents—if not as a baby, then certainly as a child, and for sure come the teenage years?

Arun had been adamant children weren't in his future.

Any more than they'd been in hers...

Oh, dear!

She saw movement beyond the glass in the terminal building and, pleased by the distraction, peered in that direction.

'It's Kam's brother, his twin—you've met him, haven't you? He's come to meet us because Kam's away.' Jane was positively bubbling with excitement. 'I didn't really expect the white robes, did you?'

Mel wasn't sure what she'd expected. Certainly not to feel her chest tighten and her heart rate zoom into dangerous arrhythmia. It must be because of the baby—it couldn't be the thought of seeing Arun.

Meeting him again…

Touching him…

Useless blob time again!

Numb brain!

She resisted the urge to slide her hand across her stomach as Jane and Bob Stapleton were bowed through a glass door into the terminal, the man in the snowy white robes—so regally erect, so noble looking, so like a desert-fantasy sheikh, Mel's knees felt weak—coming forward to introduce himself, shaking hands.

'Dr and Dr Stapleton, I am Arun Rahman al'Kawali.'

Mel stared at him—at the stranger in the white robe, barely aware of the Stapletons offering their first names and adding polite greetings.

'And, Melissa, we meet again.'

The pale green eyes she'd thought never to see again looked steadily into hers.

Would the baby have those pale, translucent-jade eyes?

'It is my great pleasure to welcome you to my country.'

He took her hand and clasped it for a moment, his warmth finding its way into her blood—heating it. Then he smiled and she knew he'd felt her reaction—not only felt it but had taken pleasure from it, seeing it as confirmation that the magic still worked between them.

And, no doubt, supposing their affair could be resumed…

Oh, dear!

Again she had to stop herself touching the barely there bulge, while her thoughts whirled uselessly through her head. I'm still attracted to him. I should have told him about the baby. What will he think—say?

Oh, dear!

'I hope while you are here I will be able to show you the beauty of the desert.'

He was watching her closely as he spoke, and Mel wondered how much of her confusion was obvious. But, whatever he read in her face, she could read nothing in his, and now he turned back to the Stapletons.

'When we met in Hawaii with water everywhere, Melissa told me of her love of the ocean. I tried to describe the desert as something similar, but I know it is too hard for those who have not seen it to understand the similarities.'

He sounded so casual, so silky smooth, so in control—but why wouldn't he? This was his country, he was the king—or half-king, sharing, Jen had said in an email, rule with his twin.

But it was the message implicit in the 'show you the desert' remark that was making Mel's anxiety levels spiral upwards—the message that now fate had brought them back together there was no reason for their affair *not* to resume.

To make matters worse, her body had not only received the message but had responded to it, getting hot and bothered and jittery right on cue.

Oh, dear!

She had to stop thinking like that. It was so negative, so weak, so utterly useless!

But what else could she think, with a brain like curdled blancmange?

For one mad instant she considered running back towards the plane. To escape to somewhere—

anywhere—until she'd worked out once and for all just how to tackle the task that lay ahead.

But to run was cowardice and she'd never been a coward, so she stiffened her body and with it her resolve, and met his silky smoothness with her own.

'I would love to see the desert,' she responded, albeit a little late. 'And I'm sure Bob and Jane are looking forward to it, too.'

His gaze slid towards her and a small smile twisted his lips. He nodded, as if to acknowledge her point, but she doubted he'd conceded it.

Not this man! Even as she'd met him in Hawaii, in Western clothes, another specialist among many, he'd exuded an aura of power, an otherness that set him apart. Quietly spoken, yet he'd been able to command attention, waiters falling over themselves to serve him before others were served, hotel staff happy to provide any service for him, people deferring to him purely because of his presence.

So, would he act as desert tour guide for all three of them?

Probably, because he was also scrupulously polite.

But would that be all Mel saw of the desert in his company?

She didn't think so.

Although she could refuse to go—refuse to accompany him anywhere. That way she'd be safe from the riot his presence was causing in her senses, the long robes he wore no barrier to attraction.

But how could they discuss the baby if she wasn't ever alone with him?

Oh, damn and blast...

'If you come this way,' he was saying, leading Bob Stapleton towards a waiting customs official. 'Your luggage will be checked here and we can go out to the car. It's parked at the side door so you can avoid the crowds.'

Crowds might have helped, Mel thought. I could have disappeared into them, never to be seen again.

Leaving Jenny short one bridesmaid?

Not possible.

So she just had to hide the surge of renewed attraction rattling her body and numbing her brain, hide a small matter of a pregnancy—thank heaven she'd dressed in deference to the country's traditions—until she had time to talk privately to him. In the meantime she would have to carry on as if Arun really was nothing more than a chance-met colleague at a medical conference.

If he could do it, so could she.

This resolve faltered as he ushered the Stapletons towards the customs official and slid close to her side.

'You are well? I cannot tell you how delighted I am that you are here in my country. There is so much I can show you, so much we can enjoy.'

The husky voice with its patent delight and suggestive undertones further weakened her resolve, but she refused to be seduced by husky voices or suggestive undertones—or by the pathetic behaviour of her body.

'You don't have to put yourself out for me,' she said. 'I know how busy you must be, with all the changes happening at the hospital. I know we'll be seeing each other from time to time, but—'

'Ah, you do not wish our affair to be resumed? Is that what you're telling me?'

No huskiness in his voice now, although a strand of steel ran through the words.

Mel tried for a really, really casual shrug and hoped she'd pulled it off.

'I'm not here long, so really there's no point.'

'Ah!' he said again, but this time there was more understanding in it. 'If that is how you feel, Melissa…'

If only he hadn't said her name. If only the word hadn't brought back such memories. Arun whispering it, softly sibilant, as he caressed her body, or shouting it, triumphant, in the throes of love-making.

She could feel the coolness as he drew away from her, all his attention back on the Stapletons.

So what was this? Arun pondered as he watched the customs officer open the first suitcase. Oh, he got the literal meaning—their affair would not be resumed—but surely there was a subtext here, hidden from him the way her luscious, ripe, curvaceous body was hidden behind the soft folds of the all-concealing gown she wore.

Maybe she was embarrassed by the proximity of the Stapletons—unable to respond to him because of their presence.

But, no, she'd spoken plainly—there'd be no point…

He studied her as she opened her suitcase, noticing faint lines of strain in her pale face.

Tiredness from the flight or something else?

He wondered why he was considering it—why he was concerned she might be tired or stressed…

Because the memories of their time together had haunted his dreams for the last four months?

Or because he cared more for her as a person than he'd allowed himself to admit?

Impossible! It had been an enjoyable affair, nothing more.

A very enjoyable affair…

The customs official gave the bags a cursory examination and another official stamped the passports, then the porter wheeled the baggage towards the car, Arun escorting Bob Stapleton while behind him he could hear Melissa chatting quietly to Jane.

They settled into the big limousine, the three guests fitting comfortably in the back seat while Arun rode beside the driver in the front. He pointed out the landmarks in the city, naming the new hotels that had sprouted from the ground to accommodate first visiting oilmen and now the tourists who came to marvel at the desert and the facilities oil money could provide.

'Oh!'

Melissa's cry made him turn and he saw her pointing, wide-eyed with wonder, towards the west, where the sinking sun was reflecting the red of the desert into the sky, so it looked like a molten golden orb in a sea of red. Closer to them the rounded dome and tall spire of a citadel stood silhouetted blackly against the red glow, and through the visitor's eyes Arun saw again the daily magic of a desert sunset.

He spoke quietly to the driver, who turned off the main highway, taking them to a vantage point from which they could watch the final glories of the day.

'I can't believe the beauty of it,' Melissa whispered, as much to herself as to those accompanying her. 'I thought the sunsets over the river where I grew up were the most beautiful in the world. I never imagined a desert sunset could be like this.'

She turned from the view towards Arun.

'And you're right, it does remind me of the ocean.'

Wonder warmed her voice, and this, more than her physical presence, started Arun's body stirring again. They'd matched so well, enjoyed each other's company so much it had gone beyond sex in that brief interlude, although both of them had known from the start that had been all it was. He'd explained he had no intention of ever marrying again—had even spoken of Hussa, his wife, and the tragedy of that gentle and beautiful young woman's death—while Melissa had admitted to being married to her job, and to finding all the satisfaction she needed in her life in the work she did with very fragile infants.

So why was she upset that they'd met again? Why could they not be friends, if not lovers?

Inwardly, he laughed. As if that would be likely, with the fire that had flared between them. One touch, he was willing to bet, and it would flame again.

Just one touch…

'Jenny?'

Jane Stapleton's gentle reminder made him realise the nightly show was finished, the sky having changed from red to gold to pink and purple and now was a darkening blue. He spoke to the driver and they continued towards the family compound.

Shaken by the beauty she had witnessed, Mel sat quietly. How could she remain stiff and un-yielding, impervious to all around her, when all around her was new and exciting, and so unex-pectedly beautiful? But if she opened herself up to the experience, might not Arun slip in as well?

She stole a glance towards him. The pristine

white scarf that covered his head was kept in place by two black twisted braids held together with a binding of gold thread. At the front, the pinpoint corners of the scarf fell to hide most of his face so all she saw, as he turned again towards the Stapletons, acting the perfect tourist guide, was his profile—the strong beak of a nose, the determined chin, and between them a glimpse of the lips she knew could fire her body to melting point.

In Western clothing, he'd been exotic, the most fantastic-looking man she'd ever seen, but in the robes—it was as if they spread an aura around him, a sense of command, of power, of…

Reined-in, hidden sexuality?

Don't think about him! Concentrate on the tour. The alley leading off that main street was the souk—the market—which accounted for the teeming crowds pushing down the narrow passageway.

'We will go there tomorrow,' he promised. 'During the day it is not so crowded and you will be more comfortable. And now here we are.'

They were approaching a corner where two

high walls met, the area lit by bright lights both inside and outside the wall. They drove along one side until they came to a huge gate, hastily pulled open by two men who had been dozing by the wall.

Inside was another world, the courtyard they entered as bright as daylight, so the beautifully laid-out gardens and ornamental pools were clearly visible.

'You will wish to see your daughter immediately,' Arun said. 'She has been living in the women's house but has moved into the house she will share with Kam after her marriage, so all three of you can stay with her.'

'The women's house?' Melissa echoed, and Arun turned so she saw all of his face.

'It is custom,' he said. 'Strange to outsiders but it has worked this way for thousands of years, although, of course, in times gone by, they were tents, not houses.'

The bland explanation told Mel he'd got the message that what they'd shared was definitely in the past. He was as mentally removed from

her as his body was behind the all-concealing gown.

So why did she feel a tremor of disappointment?

The car pulled up in front of one of the many
large houses surrounding the courtyard. Long,
shallow steps leading to a cloistered entrance
where sandals were lined up outside marked the
custom of the land.

Mel followed the Stapletons up the steps, but
at the top, as she bent to remove her shoes, Arun
touched her arm.

'Perhaps they would like some time alone,
the family. If you wish, I will show you around
the gardens.'

She studied him for a moment, knowing he'd
probably read the situation correctly—Jen *would*
like some time alone with her parents—but was
wary of his offer.

He waved an arm towards the gardens.

'We will walk through here to the stables. As
you see, there are plenty of people around so I
am unlikely to—what is the expression?—jump
on your bones?'

Another tremor sneaked through Mel's body, but this time it wasn't disappointment. Memories of the times he had 'jumped her bones' and she his brought a rush of warmth to her face, and she adjusted her shawl more closely around her face, hoping he hadn't noticed.

He took her silence for assent and led her back down the steps, then turned so they walked along a gravel path, neatly raked into intricate whorls and patterns, between perfectly manicured hedges that formed a border for the still ponds that ran down the centre of the courtyard.

The houses on either side were mirrored in them, so everywhere there were buildings, but above all a sense of calm and peace.

So calm, so peaceful, Mel was reluctant to ruin it with a declaration of her pregnancy. Although she'd have to tell him some time, and the sooner the better.

'You will explain?' Arun had touched her arm to guide her on to a side path leading between two of the sparkling pools, and now slowed his steps to ask the question.

Had he read her mind?

Did he know there was something she had to say?

Half her brain worried over this while the other half shrieked, Not here, not yet. You're tired and confused…

That half won!

'Explain?'

'This is awkward for you—the two of us meeting again? You are embarrassed?'

Could she lie—nod her head—let him believe embarrassment was the reason for her lack of response to him?

Of course she couldn't. Lies became too complicated.

'I'm not embarrassed,' she said, then realised she had no other explanation to offer for her behaviour. Not right now—not until she'd sorted it all out in her head.

Like that was going to happen!

'You have a new man in your life?' Arun persisted, no doubt seeking some valid reason for the fact that the magic which had brought them together was well and truly dead as far as she was concerned.

If only he knew how far *that* was from the truth! How skittery her skin was, and how her nerves were jumping like circus fleas.

'No,' she managed, offered what she hoped was an acceptable a smile. 'Commitment-phobe, remember?'

Arun nodded, but was obviously not satisfied.

'Your job? You had hoped to get a place on the team in Boston, had been interviewed and told you'd done well, yet you have flown here from Australia. You didn't get it? You are disappointed?'

This was getting worse. So bad, in fact, Mel had to smile—a proper smile this time—accompanied by a shake of her head, although she'd better not do that too often or she'd lose her scarf.

'Does there have to be a reason?' she asked, stopping by a still pool and lowering her body to sit on the edge of it so she could trail her hands in the water—cool her blood. 'Does your pride demand a valid excuse as to why a woman might not want to leap back into bed with you?'

The barb struck home, leaving Arun speechless—but only momentarily.

'I was not aware I'd offered you my bed,' he said, denying all the urges his body had been feeling since she'd stepped out the door of the plane. 'I was speaking more of friendship. But if your unwillingness to commit extends even to friendship, I am sorry for you.'

The light was good enough for him to see the colour leave her cheeks, and the blue eyes raised to his were stricken. She reached up and touched his arm, her wet fingers leaving damp marks on his robe.

'No, I'm the one who's sorry, Arun. It's just…'

The stricken look had been replaced by a plea. For understanding? How could he offer that when he had no idea what was going on?

How could he understand when the strong woman he remembered seemed—brittle? Vulnerable?

Surely not!

Then she smiled again, a weak effort, but it still had the effect of lighting up her face.

'Can I plead jet-lag for not being terribly coherent right now?'

She could, but he wouldn't believe her. This woman could think clearly—could even deliver a brilliant lecture at a high-level symposium—after a night of passion had prevented all consideration of sleep, so he doubted a trifle like jet-lag would faze her.

He settled beside her on the low balustrade, and leaned towards her, aware they were now completely alone in this side courtyard, aware he could kiss her.

'Is that all you want to plead?' he asked, remembering their love-making so vividly he could feel his body harden.

Another wavery smile.

'At the moment,' she said, 'but later, tomorrow, or after the wedding. Later we'll talk.'

'That's a promise?'

He'd leaned closer and she hadn't edged away, but her nod was distinctly nervous.

'Here in Zaheer we seal promises with a kiss,' he whispered.

He didn't give her time to protest, his head moving the couple of inches necessary for him capture her lips, to feel her mouth open to his demands, to taste her, to test the warm cavern of her mouth—to claim her with a kiss.

CHAPTER TWO

SURELY sheikhs shouldn't be doing this kind of thing in their own courtyard! That was Mel's first desperate thought.

Thank heavens they were both sitting so the bump kind of disappeared into her lap, was her second.

Then the heat Arun's kisses had generated from the beginning burnt through her and she gave in to sensation. Her breasts tingled, her bones turned to jelly, her insides to liquid, and she quivered with the need that only he had ever made her feel.

Damn it all, this was the last thing she wanted to happen, yet here she was responding to him like some sex-starved virgin. Well, maybe not a virgin, but certainly sex-starved…

She kissed him back, though she knew she shouldn't, revealing her need, admitting the power he had over her. Although the harsh sound of his indrawn breaths suggested she held equal power over him.

Shared passion! It had been so new to her four months ago—so new and so exciting, like exploring a different world.

If only…

Cool air brushed across her damp, kiss-sensitised lips and she realised he'd moved away. Not only moved away but was standing up, looking down at her.

'So it isn't that the attraction's died,' he said quietly, and though his face was shadowed she knew his green eyes, pale and clear, would be studying her intently, trying to read beyond whatever stunned expression might be plastered across her face, to fathom what lay beneath.

To feelings…

Or was she imagining that? Would he even care about her feelings?

'No,' she said, answering his question, not her

thoughts, for he was a sensitive man and *would* care about her feelings.

'Good,' he replied, then took her hand to help her to her feet. 'I'll take you to Jenny now. You are right. You will be busy. The excitement of the wedding has been building in the women's house all week, for all that Jenny says it's just a formality.'

He led her back to the large building where he'd left the Stapletons, introducing her to a young woman who met them at the door, telling Mel her luggage would already be in her room and Keira would show her where that was.

But Keira wasn't needed, for Jenny came bursting out of a side room into the huge vestibule.

'Mel! I thought Arun had whisked you away on the back of a camel, and was even now riding across the desert with his prisoner in true desert warrior style.'

Mel glanced at Arun before crossing the room to greet her friend. She could see the desert warrior in him today—and being carried off across the desert wasn't all that unappealing an idea...

Aaargh!

She *had* to get her head sorted!

'I'm a horse man, Jenny,' he was saying, but he smiled warmly as he spoke, as if Jenny was already someone special in his life.

'Mel rides,' Jenny told him. 'Mel, you should see the stable and the horses. They are beautiful. You'll love them. Arun rides most mornings, don't you, Arun?'

They had reached each other, and kissed cheeks, Mel careful not to get into a full hug, although her bump was hardly recognisable as pregnancy. Now Jen was standing with her arm around Mel's shoulders and matchmaking so obviously Mel knew she was blushing.

She looked from Arun's expressionless face to her friend's, glowing with happiness and excitement. 'I doubt I'll have time for riding for a few days at least,' Mel said, letting Arun off the hook, although he'd hardly rushed in and offered to take her riding. 'We've got a wedding to get ready for, remember?'

'If you wish to ride—' Arun began, and Mel had to laugh.

'You're far too late making that offer,' she teased, pleased the riding conversation had eased the tension she'd been feeling. 'And I understand, I really do. When I lived with my grandmother I rode a lot and, though cousins and friends often rode with me, there was never anything quite as good as riding on my own. Especially early in the morning, the dew still on the grass, and the world smelling fresh and new again. Just me and the horse and the countryside. I can understand your reluctance to have company.'

He smiled and she was sorry she'd relaxed her guard, for the return tease in that smile crept through her already crumbling defences.

'With me it's the horse and the desert,' he said quietly. 'And a way to sort out the problems of the world when my brain is first awake and my senses alert to everything around me.'

His smile broadened as he added, 'Well, what I really think about are the problems of the hospital, and some of the problems of our country—not quite all the world.'

'But *your* world, the one that matters to you,' Mel reminded him, and was pleased to see she'd surprised him for he looked at her for a long moment before nodding agreement.

'I'll leave you now,' Arun said, and turned away. Not a moment too soon, he decided as he stopped outside the door to slip his feet into his sandals. It was all right to be physically attracted to Melissa Cartwright, and he'd enjoyed her sharp mind and probing intelligence as well as her body when they'd had their brief affair. But he didn't like the feeling that she might be in tune with his emotions or keying in to his thoughts. Such intimate closeness was the one thing he'd avoided since Hussa's death.

Jenny led Mel into a vast room, adorned with ancient tapestries, bright rugs, soft sofas and thick cushions. But the immediate impression was of colour—reds and golds, pinks and purples, unlikely mixes of geometric and floral designs, hidden corners behind drapes and screens. It was like something out of a fairy-tale, and Mel paused as her senses struggled to take it all in.

Bob and Jane Stapleton were sitting on a long leather ottoman, studying something that looked like a map. In front of them a low table was laden with platters of fruit, nuts, cheeses, bread, and small cake-like delicacies.

'Come,' Jenny said. 'You need to eat and drink and I'm dying to tell you all my adventures. Then, when Mum and Dad have gone to bed, you can tell me all of yours.'

She paused and turned to study Mel, touching her hand to her face.

'You're well? Things are all right with you?'

Mel knew she was searching for disappointment—or perhaps some hint of a reason why Mel was not working in the hospital in Boston, in the job of her dreams. But the answer lay not in her face but in the shape of her body…

'We'll talk later,' Mel confirmed, although she knew she couldn't talk to Jenny—not properly—not until she'd told Arun.

But *how* could she tell him?

How could she explain why she hadn't told him earlier?

She followed Jenny across the room, hearing, and envying, the happiness in her friend's voice, although if anyone deserved happiness, it was Jenny.

Mel joined the Stapletons on the ottoman, took a damp scented napkin from a young girl standing behind her and wiped her hands, then picked up a plate and carefully chose a few of the exotic delicacies to try.

'I'm not really hungry,' she protested, when Jenny urged her to have more. 'They kept feeding us on the flight.'

'But you should drink something to keep up your fluid level. Try this juice, it's made from dates. You'll love it.'

Then, having urged food and drink onto her friend, she settled back to tell her tale.

'So I thought, loving him as I did, that marrying Kam just wasn't possible,' Jenny said, much later, coming to the end of the saga of her romance. 'He was the new ruler, he would need heirs and I didn't know…'

She pressed her hand to her stomach and all three of her listeners understood the gesture—remembering the pain and grief Jenny had suffered when she'd lost her husband and unborn son in a car accident. Worse still had been the news from the doctors who had pieced her back together again. They had doubted she would be able to have another child.

But Jen's face was still glowing—*and* she was marrying Kam—so obviously her possible inability to produce an heir no longer worried her.

'And *that* was when Arun made his offer,' she finished triumphantly, beaming at her listeners as if this was the most wonderful news she'd ever imparted to anyone.

Their blank stares must have told her something, for she laughed.

'Sorry. You don't understand. Kam had told me something of Arun's past, you see. Arun married when he was young—his wife was a beautiful young woman called Hussa. He was working in the city while she stayed, as was the custom in their father's time, in the women's house in the family compound in the country. She was young and very shy and when she had pains in her stomach she didn't like to tell anyone, and by the time someone realised she was sick her appendix had burst, peritonitis had set in, and she died before anyone could save her.'

'That's terrible, but it does still happen in this day and age,' Jane said. 'Even back home, when people put the stomach pain down to something they ate, and the resulting infection resists drug therapy.'

Jenny nodded her agreement.

'Arun, naturally enough,' she continued, 'was devastated, and swore he'd never marry again. He's so like Kam and yet so different. Kam calls him a playboy, although I'm sure he's not that bad, but I could understand him not wanting to marry again.'

Mel, contrarily eager to hear more about Arun, had followed the story avidly, but surely it wasn't finished. She glanced at Jane and Bob, who looked equally puzzled.

'And Arun's offer?' Mel prompted, and Jen smiled again—smiled radiantly.

'He said not to worry, he'd marry and have children who could be heirs, and my reason for not wanting to marry Kam was swept away.'

'Oh, dear' was no longer strong enough. What Mel needed was a really bad expletive, but her grandmother had been extremely old-fashioned as far as even the mildest of swear words was concerned, and though Mel had heard plenty as a student, and still did in Theatre, she could rarely bring herself to use one.

Not even in her head!

But this was a disaster. She could hardly present Arun with her news when he was seeking a new wife, maybe already arranging to be married.

But he also wanted a child…

Their child?

Impossible!

Jen was still speaking and Mel tried to focus on what she was saying. She'd learn what she could then later she could work out where to go next.

'You have to understand that things are done

differently here,' Jenny explained. 'People still follow the traditions of hundreds of years ago, so a marriage of convenience, like Arun offered to organise for himself, is not unusual.'

'And has he done this? Organised it?' Mel hoped her voice sounded stronger than it felt as she croaked the question out past taut vocal cords. She also hoped the questions sounded natural, under the circumstances.

Apparently they did, for Jenny smiled.

'He hasn't said so, but knowing the way he and Kam work—think of something, get it done—I imagine he has it well in hand. In fact, I wouldn't have been surprised if he'd suggested a double wedding.'

'Oh, I'm sure he wouldn't want to take anything away from your big day,' Jane said, and Jenny laughed.

'Mum, it's not really a big day. Kam and I feel married already. This is just a ceremony for the family and an excuse for the local people to party. Although Kam's tried to explain things to me, and I understand a few words of the local language, the four of us will know nothing of what's going on.'

Jane looked doubtful but Bob was made of sterner stuff.

'As long as you're happy,' he said gruffly, 'and I can see you are, that's all that matters. Now, when do we meet this man of yours?'

Mel watched the colour rise in Jenny's cheeks and knew Bob had spoken the truth. Jenny was truly happy.

'Tomorrow night. We're having a big dinner. It's traditional the day before the wedding, although I shouldn't be attending it. But times are changing and I'll be there. Kam will be back from the refugee camp.' She turned to Mel. 'He took the new doctor up there a couple of days ago and was staying to see he'd settled in. You'll all meet him tomorrow.'

It became a signal for movement, the Stapletons deciding they were ready to retire and Jenny rising to see them to their room.

'You stay right there,' she said to Mel. 'We need to talk.'

But when Mel thought about what that talk would entail she shook her head. Better a small deceit than a larger one.

'I think our talk will have to wait, Jen,' she said. 'I'm bushed. Must be jet-lag.'

Jen's look was disbelieving but she didn't argue, leading all three of them back through the wide entrance, taking her parents to one room then showing Mel towards another further down a corridor.

'This small place is going to be your and Kam's house?' Mel teased. 'I should be dropping breadcrumbs so I can find my way back to the front door.'

'Keira will show you where to go. She will be your personal attendant while you're here, and will be sleeping in a little alcove off your room, so anything you want, just ask.'

'In English, or do I need a few words of Zaheer?'

Jenny smiled.

'Kam and Arun have made sure all the attendants—I know that's a strange word but they are more like family than servants, although they serve the family—have had good schooling, and that includes learning English. The twins have also paid tuition costs for any of the younger ones who want to go to university, whether here or overseas.'

As if to confirm Jenny's words, Keira was waiting in the room—far too large to be called a bedroom—set aside for Mel.

'I have unpacked for you,' she said, in clear, un-accented English. 'You would like a drink of some-thing, tea perhaps, or milk, before you go to bed?'

'No, I'm fine,' Mel told her, following the young girl into a splendidly opulent bathroom, admiring its beauty, then assuring Keira she could manage to shower on her own.

Shower and shroud herself in her voluminous nightgown—she certainly didn't want word of her pregnancy spreading through the house before she'd told Arun.

Or Jenny!

She slipped into the big bed, feeling the softness of the sheets—surely not silk—wondering how Jen must feel, living in this house after her years in tents and mud huts in war-torn countries or refugee camps.

Not that luxury would change Jen...

But as hard as she tried to concentrate on Jenny and her future in this country, Mel's mind kept slipping back to Arun and to the new dilemma she now faced—his approaching marriage...

And as she listened to a distant clock chime three times, she decided. She would stop thinking about it, stop putting it off, just get up in the morning, go out to the stables where she knew he'd be, and tell him.

Let him decide what he wanted to do with the knowledge...

Arun was leading Saracen out of the stables when he saw her approaching, an anxious Keira by her side.

'Melissa?'

He paused, aware of many things. In the kind, pearly light of dawn she looked pale and tired, yet his body still responded to her.

Her usual confident stride was hesitant, and now, as she drew nearer, he read indecision in her face.

'You wish to ride?'

She shook her head, then nodded.

'I know you prefer to ride alone, but I thought...'

She stopped and looked around in a desperate fashion, as if seeking escape from the compound.

'I'd be happy to have you accompany me.' Good manners had saved him in many an awkward situation and this, with the confident Melissa looking positively haunted, could be classed as a very awkward one.

'I'm not really dressed for it. Didn't think to bring jeans or jodhpurs, thinking they might not be acceptable...'

Arun took in the loose trousers and tunic Melissa was wearing, not regular riding gear but surely unexceptional. He glanced towards Keira, wondering if something in her expression might shed some light on Melissa's uncertainty, but

Keira's face was devoid of all expression, although doubtless she was wondering if all foreigners were as strange as this woman she was watching over.

'If you don't mind me riding with you, that might be best,' Melissa finally said, and Arun called back into the stable for one of the men to saddle Mershinga, a gentle mare his sisters often rode.

'It will be my pleasure,' Arun said, then he added to Keira, 'I will return Dr Cartwright to the house later.'

The young woman nodded and departed, Melissa turning to watch her move away before swinging back towards Arun.

'Maybe we shouldn't ride—maybe we could just go somewhere and talk,' she said, the words rushing out in a super-fast stream, as if she needed to get them said.

Saracen, perhaps picking up tension in the air, began to prance and Arun soothed him with a hand against his neck and a few quiet words.

Would that such a touch would soothe the visitor!

He handed Saracen's bridle to a young boy who was hovering nearby and stepped towards her.

'Melissa,' he said, coming close enough to see the evidence of a sleepless night in the blue-tinged shadows beneath her eyes, taking her hands gently in his. 'Come ride with me. Relax. Enjoy the desert. Later, if you wish, we will talk, but for now forget your cares and concerns and let the rhythm of a horse and the clean morning air of the desert work their magic.'

He touched his fingers to her chin and tipped her head so he could look into her eyes.

Then regretted it, for what he saw was anguish—an anguish so deep it touched his heart and made him want to hold her against his body, hold her safe in his arms, and promise her that everything would be all right.

Some promise, when he didn't know what ailed her—what was causing her such distress.

'Come!' he said instead, taking her hand and leading her to where another young man held the pale grey mare. 'This is Mershinga. She will carry you surely and safely.'

He held the horse's head while Melissa lifted herself lightly into the saddle, then he adjusted the stirrups for her, being careful not to let his hand linger on her ankle—on any part of her—for, in spite of his knowledge of her troubled state, he still felt the attraction between them.

Surely and safely! Arun's words repeated themselves in Mel's head. Maybe Arun was right. Maybe she could just ride and enjoy the sensation of freedom being on a horse always brought her—the wind in her hair, the morning sun on her skin and the new experience of the desert. She could let the magic of a new day work on the tensions that had tormented her all night.

Then later—some other time—she'd talk to Arun…

He had mounted his horse, a bold, black stallion who frisked and gambolled as if reminding the rider who was the boss. But Arun held him under control, letting him prance a little but always reining him back in. You are not the boss, his strong but slender hands were signalling.

And as Mel watched the tussle between horse and rider, her own mount following sedately behind the pair, she did relax, her taut muscles loosening, her body adjusting the rhythm of the mare's gait, her lungs welcoming the crisp morning air.

They left the compound through a smaller gate than the one the car had entered the previous evening, and to Mel's delight were immediately in the desert.

'It's so close,' she marvelled, as Arun reined in his still fidgety mount and waited for her to come alongside. 'I thought we'd have to follow roads or paths to the outskirts of the city.'

Arun smiled at her.

'This *is* the outskirts of the city. From here the desert stretches out towards those mountains, and in the other direction to an inland sea.'

He pointed to the mountains, indistinct behind a gauzy morning haze. They were like a metaphor for this place—veiled mountains, veiled women, curtains and screens—secrets.

'You wish to canter? You are confident enough on Mershinga?'

'Yes!'

Mel smiled as she replied, suddenly longing for a canter—for a gallop, in fact—to blow the cobwebs from her head. The secret wouldn't change for being kept a little longer.

They went slowly at first, no doubt because Arun wanted to see the level of her riding skills, but then he turned and raised his eyebrows at her.

'Faster?' he asked.

'Faster,' she agreed, loosening the reins and digging her heels into the mare's sides, taking off beside him, although the stallion soon outpaced her mount.

She caught up with him at what looked like a cairn of some kind, stones stacked on top of each other beside some squat palms.

'Is this an oasis?' she asked, not bothering to hide the disappointment she felt. Where was the water? Did three date palms count as lush forestation?

He laughed.

'A very small one, but none the less important if you were a traveller in the desert. Come, dismount and try the water. I can assure you that the most expensive bottled water in the world will not compare in purity or taste.'

He vaulted easily off his horse as he was speaking and looped the reins over a post beside the cairn, then held the mare's head while Mel dismounted.

Leaving the mare untethered, her reins knotted loosely to they wouldn't trail on the ground, he led Mel towards a small well she hadn't noticed.

'This is a wadi—a place where one of the underground streams beneath the desert runs close enough to the surface for the palms to grow and for the people, in ancient times, to dig a well.'

He threw the wooden bucket that was sitting on top of the well wall down into the depths, then wound the handle to bring it back up, crystal-clear water splashing from it.

Cupping his hands, he dipped them into the water then offered them to Mel.

She drank, more out of politeness than thirst, then drank again for the water was as special as he had said.

'You're right, it's better than any water I've ever tasted.' Then she looked up into his face and laughed, surprising herself as her inner tension had been so great a laugh was the last thing she'd expected to issue from her lips. 'That sounds stupid, doesn't it? Water doesn't really have a taste.'

Arun grinned at her.

'No more stupid than me telling you it tasted better than any other water on earth,' he agreed, dipping his hands in again and drinking himself.

Mel watched him, the handsome man in jeans and sweatshirt, water running down his stubbly chin, staining the front of his shirt.

Her baby's father...

'I'm pregnant.'

The words came out before she could prevent them. So much for all the phrases she'd prac-tised during the night, all the lead-in explana-tions and excuses!

She studied him, reading puzzlement in the face he raised towards her, then disbelief as it dawned on him why she should be blurting out such a thing—to him of all people.

'How pregnant?'

A crisp demand for clarification. Her stomach coiled in on itself at the coldness in his voice.

'Four months.'

'Impossible! I took precautions! Every—'

He stopped and she saw him frown as he thought back. Would he pick up on the memory she'd had when she'd discovered her pregnancy?

They'd opted out of a formal dinner, deciding instead to dine at a small, local, beachside restaurant someone had recommended, eating lobster on a deck beside the sea, wiping the butter from each other's chins with gentle fingers. Then walking back to the hotel along the beach—the secluded cove, the midnight swim, making love in the warm, enveloping water of the Pacific Ocean.

'And, presuming you're telling me now because it's my child, you're also telling me that for four months you've felt no need to tell me? Seen no reason to share this information?'

Arun paused, studying the woman in front of him, aware how pale and fragile she was looking, yet he was so angry—so enraged—he could no more stop himself from hurting her than he could turn back time four months.

'Would you have told me at all had not Jenny's wedding brought you to Zaheer? Or, having seen the compound, are you after money?'

He saw her wince, although he could tell from the way she'd stiffened she'd tried desperately hard to stop the reaction, but he couldn't afford to feel sympathy for her, not when she'd kept such information to herself all this time.

Not when he was finding it difficult to process that same information—to work out how he felt and what it meant to him.

'Arun,' she began, moving so she could sit down on the stone seat at the cairn, her hands twisting in her lap. 'I know this is a shock—you have to believe it was just as great a shock to me. And, yes, I should have told you earlier.'

Blue eyes, dark with remorse and what seemed like a shadow of fear, looked pleadingly up into his.

'But I had no idea how to react myself,' she admitted quietly. 'I didn't know how to think, what to do.'

She paused, then added, 'I was terrified.'

So the shadow *was* fear, but why?

And surely terror was something of an over-reaction!

She'd bowed her head, as if his scrutiny after such an admission was too much for her to bear.

But how could he not pursue it?

'Terrified?'

For a moment he thought his query would be ignored, but eventually she raised her head, and tried on a smile so pathetic it wrung his heart.

'Stupid, isn't it? I can operate on newborn babies without a twinge of fear.'

And now he understood—or thought he did—he sat down beside her and took her hand.

'You were frightened the baby might have something wrong with it? A congenital defect? That's not surprising, Melissa, considering your work.'

But she shook her head, and withdrew her

hand from his, standing up, putting distance between them, pacing around the three trees she'd derided earlier.

'I was terrified about the pregnancy.'

She paused, as if startled by her own honesty, then rushed into qualifying statements, that to Arun's ears rang true yet not entirely true at the same time.

'What did I, brought up by a strict but fair and very proper grandmother, know about bringing up a child? Then there were the problems of single motherhood, not to mention juggling work and a baby. It all seemed to crash down on me until I couldn't think at all. So I didn't! I blotted it from my mind—pretended it wasn't happening, told no one, not even Jenny—thinking that once I'd calmed down I'd be able to break it down like any other task into doable-sized pieces and work out all the answers.'

She sighed then sat down again.

'That didn't happen. Even now, when I try to think about it, my mind goes blank—or turns to mush! I know this is a stupid reaction, Arun, and I'm only telling you because it might help you understand why I didn't contact you about the pregnancy earlier. Oh, I had all kinds of other excuses—I might lose the baby; you hadn't wanted a child, or any kind of commitment, so it didn't matter if you didn't know—but the truth is I tried to pretend to myself it wasn't happening, and if I didn't talk about it, the pretence was easier.'

He could feel her tension, the trembling in her body, and knew what she said she felt was real—stripped bare of any pretence—although he sensed there was a lot more left unsaid.

And was it that—the fact she was holding something back—that stifled any sympathy for her? That fed his anger?

'If that was how you felt, why didn't you terminate the pregnancy?' The words were harsh, doing nothing to hide his anger or his simmering suspicion.

She swung towards him, disbelief in her face.

'Why didn't I what?' she demanded, steeling herself and meeting his anger with her own.

'Terminate the pregnancy,' he repeated, each word as cold and hard as a chip of ice.

'How could I when I *save* children's lives? That's my *life,* it's what I do! I'm not against abortion and I can understand, in a lot of circumstances, choosing to go that way, but me? How could I?'

She was so genuinely shocked he felt his anger drain away, leaving a huge void within his emotions. Understanding might have filled it, pity even, but he knew he couldn't afford either. Not until he'd thought this through.

Not until he'd actually accepted the fact that this woman was carrying his child…

'We should go back,' he said, standing up and moving towards his horse.

'That's all you have to say?'

He swung back to face her.

'You've just told me you still can't fully believe it after four months and you expect me to have some thoughts on this situation after five minutes?'

'This situation!' She echoed the words so faintly he knew he'd hurt her as badly as the slashing of a knife would have hurt her flesh.

Then she straightened her shoulders, and tilted her chin—the strong woman he'd known back in control.

'No, of course not. That was stupid of me,' she said. 'We'll go back.'

She walked across to where Mershinga waited patiently, unknotted the reins and mounted the quiet mare, the grace of her movements telling Arun how at ease she was on horseback.

And was he thinking that so he didn't have to think about her shocking revelation?

Probably!

He mounted Saracen and eased the big stallion alongside the mare.

'Boston?'

The quick glance she shot his way told him she'd understood the question. In fact, she half smiled in response, her shoulders lifting in a dismissive shrug.

'I did have enough functioning brain cells to realise that was impossible. As soon as I knew, I contacted the team leader to tell him I couldn't take the job. Junior members of the team are on retrieval duty and could be called out at any time of the day or night, flying anywhere in the United States to collect a donor heart. Not exactly the ideal situation for a single mother.'

'You could have hired a nanny. Surely you'd have to do that anyway, if you intend to keep on working.'

Was he still thinking she was after money? Mel wondered as the cool, unemotional remark reverberated through her head.

She tried for cool and unemotional herself.

'I do intend to keep on working—somehow, some time. I have to work, not just for my own personal satisfaction but because I'm good at what I do—very good—and to me it would be criminal to not continue, considering all the time and effort other people have put in to get me to this standard. How I'll juggle things I'm not quite sure, but at least, now that I've turned down the Boston job, I have some time to consider options.'

'You're not working at the moment? Not at all?'

Mel breathed deeply, though she was barely aware of the desert air. It was more a relieved kind of deep breath. Talking work was so much easier than talking babies.

'I'd resigned, knowing I was going. Lately, I've been doing on-call work—filling in for colleagues taking leave—making up an extra pair of hands when a team is short. The hospital where I'd been working wants me back, but...'

How to explain that she couldn't commit to full-time work right now? How to explain her determination that the child she carried would have a loving, at-home mother, not a part-time carer or a nanny, at least for the first months of its life?

How to explain anything when thinking that far ahead brought on the insane, irrational terror, so strongly felt it verged on a panic attack?

CHAPTER THREE

ARUN tried not to glance towards her as they rode back to the compound, but his gaze drifted sideways, seeking a change of body shape beneath the loose tunic top Melissa wore.

Nothing!

Which was hardly surprising.

What was surprising was his need to see the shape—his need for confirmation—as if only by seeing a slight swell in her belly could he really believe this was true.

He was intelligent to know this was his mind's way of putting off the moment when it had to consider exactly what this pregnancy meant to him, and for his mind and emotions to adjust to the fact that this woman was carrying his child.

If he could hold onto his anger—justified, surely, by her failure to tell him—it might help, but the anger was already fading, giving way to a kind of free-floating confusion, a state of mind foreign to him in recent years.

And if he was confused, how must Melissa feel—the career-woman with the huge prize of a job in a top paediatric surgical team suddenly snatched away from her?

Although it needn't have been...

She *could* have terminated the pregnancy and no one would have been any the wiser...

The conjecture made him realise just how little he knew of her, having seen only the strong, confident, independent and undeniably sexy woman who'd won applause for her presentation at the symposium, and been spoken of as one of the up-and-coming paediatric surgeons on the world stage.

They'd reached the compound and he held Saracen back to allow the mare to enter first, watching the way Melissa sat the horse, seeing the straight back and the erect carriage of her head. She may have shown weakness when she'd told him of the baby, but he sensed she was once again in control of her emotions.

Well in control, judging from the way she dismounted then turned, looking up at him.

'I won't say anything to Jenny just yet,' she said. 'It's taken me eight weeks to get as far as I have in considering this, I can at least give you a couple of days to decide what, if anything, you want to do.'

'What, if anything, I want to do?' Arun said. His brain must be floating more freely than he'd realised for the words made no sense whatsoever.

'I'm quite prepared to raise the child myself,' Melissa added, and he wondered if she could see the confusion in his voice mirrored in his eyes, for she continued, speaking quietly, 'I know things have changed for you since we met, and that you've been making plans for marriage. I don't want to interfere with that in any way. There's no need for you to have any involvement with this child if that's the way you want it. I'm not asking for support, either physical or financial, Arun, I just knew you had to know.'

'Knew I had to know? Not have any involvement?'

New anger raised his voice, and the sound brought a couple of lads running from the stables.

'We'll talk later,' Melissa said. 'Somewhere private. When you're ready.'

But would he ever be ready? he wondered as he dismounted.

Of course he would. He just had to think it through.

And get to work—he was already late.

And organise the setting up of the new unit at the hospital while Melissa was still in Zaheer to advise him.

And get through the family celebrations this evening, then Kam's wedding tomorrow.

A piece of cake—wasn't that the saying?

Melissa was watching him, as if waiting for a reply, but he had no words for her—not right now.

'I'll go back to the house,' she said at last. 'Jenny will be wondering where I've got to.'

She had turned to go when a woman came running towards the stables, calling his name.

'Your sister, sir. They said come quickly. The baby—'

The baby? Coincidence or fate that babies were dominating the morning?

'Problems?' Melissa queried as he hesitated, trying to switch his thoughts from one baby to another. 'Is she pregnant?'

'Due next month,' Arun replied, his mind now firmly on his sister as he followed the messenger back towards the women's house.

Melissa strode beside him so he explained.

'I've been keeping a special eye on her. The foetal heartbeat has been strange. Probably more your field than mine. And, of course, in the way of sisters, she believes more of what her gynaecologist tells her than her brother. And, being a male, I've not been allowed to listen to it except through her voluminous gowns so I could be wrong.'

He was hurrying, but Melissa was keeping up with him, and part of him was glad, although he hoped with all his heart there was nothing wrong with Tia's baby—hoped that having Melissa present at the birth would prove nothing more than an unnecessary distraction.

But he wanted her there—he *knew* that!

Mel followed him back to a house beside the one she'd spent the night in—Jenny's house, although it was hard to think of it that way. This one seemed even larger, and as she slipped off her shoes she smiled to see such a variety of footwear lined up there, from tiny child-sized sandals to designer scuffs. Was this the women's house that so many people were inside?

She followed Arun in, awed by how palatial it was. Built from the same sandstone blocks as Jenny's, with most of the outer stones ornately carved into open fretwork so air and light came through, the rooms themselves were beautiful in their simplicity. But the rich rugs scattered on the floors, the satin and velvet cushions thrown around, the vibrant hangings on the walls depicting vivid hunting and battle scenes—they all contributed to an overall impression of exotic magnificence.

'Oh, Arun, the baby's coming, it's early and the doctor isn't here. What will we do?'

Arun put his arm around the small, agitated woman who'd approached him, her hands held pleadingly in front of her. He spoke to her, soothing words Mel didn't understand, then added in English, 'Have you called Jenny?'

'She's with Tia now. And Jenny's mother, who says she has delivered more babies than she can count and we are not to worry, but how can I not worry about my daughter's first baby?'

'Of course you're entitled to worry,' he said gently, then spoke again in his own language.

'And this is Melissa,' he added, switching to English. 'Jenny's friend and a baby doctor. Shall I take her in?'

'Melissa, I am Miriam, Arun's aunt. It is my daughter Tia who is having the baby.' The woman held out a small bejewelled hand and Mel shook it gently, fearing she might break such a delicate structure.

'It is bad this has happened to disrupt your first day in our country,' she continued, leading the way through the huge room then down a corridor to the right. 'But so many doctors here for my daughter must be a good thing, mustn't it? Although, of course, Kam is away and Mr Dr Stapleton has not been involved. But still four, if she allows Arun in, that is.'

Her chatter failed to hide her anxiety, and Mel understood the fear Miriam must be feeling for her daughter.

Understood it only too well. She steeled herself against her own misgivings, reminding herself of all the births she'd witnessed, the babies she'd delivered before specialising. So few women died in childbirth these days, her fear was laughable.

But laughter was a long way off…

Needing a distraction, a focus for her attention, she turned to Miriam.

'Are you hoping for a girl or a boy?' she asked. 'Or do you know?'

'We know it is a boy and this is a wonderful thing.' The awe in the words told Mel this was important, a fact reinforced when Miriam continued, taking Arun's hand and looking up into his face.

'Strange, isn't it, my Arun, that after all the years I tried to have a son and failed, and my other daughters have all had girls, yet Tia's first should be a boy.'

They entered a room large enough to be a village hall, filled, it seemed to Mel, with swathed and twittering women. One said something and they all turned, some drawing their veils close around their heads at the sight of Arun, while others wore Western apparel of jeans and T-shirts and greeted him with easy familiarity.

'I had a lot of girls,' Miriam said, slightly apologetically. 'Although, of course, not all of the women in here are my children.'

But Mel's eyes had already picked out Jen and her mother, both bent over a woman crouched in a corner of the room. Arun went directly to the corner to comfort his sister—or if her mother was his aunt maybe Mel had got the relationship wrong and the woman was his cousin. Whatever the relationship was, the young—very young— woman was obviously glad to see him, grasping his hand and bursting into tears.

'Stay with me,' she begged, her American-accented English suggesting she'd been sent to school in the US rather than England.

Mel slipped past the pair, virtually unnoticed, and touched Jenny on the shoulder.

'Is everything OK?' she asked.

Jen nodded but looked so grave Mel guessed things were far from good.

'Mel, I'm so glad you're here. The delivery is going all right—the head's crowned and she's ready to push—but I can't hear a foetal heartbeat. Your speciality may be paediatric surgery but at least you've got the paeds qualifications.'

Jane was kneeling beside the crouching woman, her hands ready to take the baby's head as soon as it was delivered, while Jen and Arun between them supported Tia as she strained to ease her baby into the world.

Melissa went to a table to one side of the action, where a jug of water and a basin had been provided for hand-washing. She used a liquid soap and wondered if germs would be the least of this new baby's worries. If Jen couldn't hear a heartbeat…

She was tipping water into the basin to rinse her hands when Tia screamed, and although Mel knew this was natural—few women gave birth silently—her heart rate accelerated and fear for the young woman made her hands shake.

Fortunately for her state of mind, the baby arrived in the next instant. Her own pregnancy was forgotten as the little boy was delivered, shown to his mother then, with the umbilical cord cut, he was swaddled in a soft cloth and Jen carried him to a side table, leaving her mother to manage the final stage of birth but signalling with her head for Mel to come closer.

'He's breathing but he's not a very satisfactory pink,' Jenny murmured to Mel, 'and his heartbeat…'

Melissa took over the examination. Many years ago a woman doctor called Virginia Apgar had worked out a scoring system for newborns and her system was still in use today. One minute after birth the infant was checked for heart rate, respiratory effort, muscle tone, response to stimuli and colour and given a score of zero, one or two for each check. The numbers were then added together. At one minute the score could still be low, but if it was still low after five minutes, the baby needed serious support.

'I'll suction him to make sure his trachea is clear, but he needs oxygen. Was the birth to be here or at a hospital? Would there be oxygen available here?' Jen shrugged and Mel turned towards Arun, who had helped his sister to her bed and was presumably explaining that all babies had to be examined after birth.

He caught her glance and left Tia with Miriam, who had followed them into the room.

'He needs oxygen—is there any on hand?' Mel asked, and was dismayed when Arun shook his head.

'Then an ambulance asap,' she added. 'We need to get him to hospital. His breathing's laboured, his heart's tachycardic, his Apgar is appalling—two at a minute and from the colour of his hands and feet it's not going to be much better at five minutes.'

'I'll get someone to call.'

But Mel had stopped listening, instead bending over the tiny baby to blow air gently into his labouring lungs, her whole being focussed on this fragile child.

Was it instinct that made Tia realise something was wrong? The woman gave a wailing cry, and struggled to get out of bed.

'I'll talk to her,' Jen said. 'You keep blowing.'

Mel didn't need this advice. The first boy baby in Miriam's family for two generations could die if she didn't keep blowing so as to maximise the oxygen his body was labouring to take in.

Arun returned as she rested two fingers on the baby's chest to check his heart again.

Arun! Childbirth! Babies!

She brushed the thoughts aside, compartmentalising her mind, *this* baby her focus now.

'What do you think?' Arun asked, handing her a stethoscope.

'I've no idea but his heartbeat's way too irregular and his breathing is so laboured he's tiring himself out and that's putting more pressure on his heart.'

She put the stethoscope to her ears and listened to the baby's chest, concentrating on the echoing sounds. The first heart sound seemed normal then she heard a recognisable click as a defective truncal valve opened, followed by a second loud and single heart sound.

'You can't diagnose on heart sounds but he definitely needs some scans and tests,' she said. 'Here, you're the cardiologist—you listen.' She handed the stethoscope to Arun.

'Not good, is it?' he said quietly. Then, removing the stethoscope, he gently palpated the tiny chest with one long, slender forefinger.

'Feel here—a systolic thrill.'

Arun reached for Melissa's hand to guide it into place, touching her as naturally as he would have any colleague, but as she nodded, her face grave, he remembered she was there as a guest—a bridesmaid for a wedding the following day.

And pregnant as well.

How could he ask for her help?

How could he not, when Tia's baby needed

the kind of help only she, right here and now, could give?

He recalled seeing her hands tremble as she'd washed them, and wondered what inner strength she must have to continue to work in her field.

She may have said it didn't worry her, but how could she not wonder if her own child was not properly formed in some way?

His child!

And standing there beside her, watching as she breathed life-giving air into his nephew's lungs, the anger he thought he had under control surged through him and he growled under his breath...

Growling wasn't getting him anywhere, so Arun tried a brisk shake of his head in an attempt to clear his brain, unable to believe these niggling thoughts had invaded it at a time like this. His mind seemed to have split into two parts, one concentrated on the baby, the other filled with questions about this woman who'd come so unexpectedly back into his life.

Terrified?

Surely that was an absurd word for her to have used.

He watched her bend over the baby, continuing to blow gently into his tiny lungs.

'I'll get him to the hospital,' he said, following the most important train of thought in his head. 'The ambulance will have to take Tia as well—there's no way she'll leave the baby,' he added as Jenny returned to the table to check on the newborn's welfare.

'You've paediatric specialists? A paediatric ICU? Surgical specialists?' Mel asked.

'Of course not,' Jenny snapped. 'The new hospital was built by greedy foreign specialists, both men and women, who wanted to make money more than they wanted to help the local population. Kam and Arun were helpless to change things before their father died, and even now progress is slow. With Tia pregnant they did start by getting some O and G staff and putting in a maternity ward and nursery. On the plus side, the hospital has first-class operating theatres, all the fancy machines you'll need to scan and image the little one, and if you have to use the ICU set-up for men and women recovering from facelifts and tummy tucks, well, at least it's got great monitors.'

Mel turned to Arun who nodded glumly.

'Our country has taken a strange route from the past to the present. In the past babies were born at home and lived or died. People got sick and they too lived or died. Gradually, as local people trained in medicine, clinics were established in the towns, where sick people could be seen by doctors and nursed if necessary. In the city there was a hospital of sorts. Then what is called progress happened and a new hospital was built, but by private investors who wanted to make money out of their investment.'

'You've a hospital that was built for the sole purpose of making money?'

Arun shrugged, but Mel felt his shame so deeply she wanted to reach out and touch his shoulder.

Far better not to touch…

'We are renovating the old hospital now, and changing things in the new one. You know I'm a cardiologist and Kam's a general surgeon,' he continued, 'and now we have physicians working there and a system of residents and registrars—but we cannot run before we walk.'

Perhaps hearing the pain in his voice as he explained, Jen took over.

'Apart from the work Kam and Arun and the new staff do, most of the surgical work is cosmetic. People come from everywhere, particularly India and Africa, to be operated on by some of the best surgeons in the world—'

'But little babies who need urgent surgery die?'

Mel broke into Jen's explanation and Arun sighed in the face of her anger.

'We fly them out to a country—a hospital— that can help them whenever we can. Kam and I have been doing that for years—using our own plane. It's not perfect, but it often saves a life.'

'Not this life,' Mel said, picking up the tiny baby and swaddling the blanket around him. 'This one needs help now. Is the ambulance here yet?'

'It should be here any minute.'

It was a statement, but Mel heard more in the words.

An unspoken plea?

She turned towards him.

'Will you travel with it?' he asked. 'Help me examine the baby? I don't like to ask it of you, a visitor to our country, but…'

Mel turned and looked into his face, so full of concern, and something that looked like embarrassment, as if he'd hated having to ask this of her—or any visitor.

'Of course I'll come,' she assured him, and now read relief in his eyes.

Had he doubted she'd help?

And could she blame him? In spite of the time they'd spent together—in spite of the child she carried—what did they know of each other?

Her thoughts were interrupted as two women in dark gowns came into the room, pushing a collapsible ambulance stretcher between them. Arun lifted the new mother onto it, explaining to her in his own language, soothing her agitation.

He accompanied the stretcher and the women attendants towards the outer door, Mel following close behind with the baby.

'You don't have to do this,' Arun said, as if uncertain she was going willingly.

'It's what I do best,' she said, and smiled at him, the smile promising that for as long as it took to get this baby stable, all other matters would be set aside.

Mel was aware of others following, but it wasn't until she climbed into the ambulance that she realised all the women who had been in the room expected to come as well. Fortunately Jenny was there to sort things out and it was she who helped the ambulance women close the doors against the thrusting, noisy crowd.

The young mother looked fearfully from Arun to the baby in Mel's arms. Arun leaned forward and put his arm around his sister, holding her close to his chest while he spoke words Mel didn't understand. But even without knowing their meaning, she could hear the understanding, support and love he was offering, along with the heart-breaking news that all was not well with her new son.

The woman responded more loudly, angry words of denial, Mel guessed, then she pushed away from Arun and lay back on the trolley, her back turned to the man who'd tried to comfort her.

'Women ambulance attendants?' Mel queried, mainly to break the awkward silence that had grown to fog-like proportions in the cabin of the vehicle, interrupted only by the soft crying of the new mother.

'You don't have them in Australia?'

'Of course we do, but I suppose because they're usually paired with men I don't notice them as different.'

Arun smiled and Mel saw again the devastating looks and charm that had swept her off her feet—and into bed—four months ago.

Felt it too, in a rising heat deep within her body…

How absurd to be feeling such…lust was surely the only name for it in an ambulance screaming through the streets of a foreign country, a tiny, fragile baby held in her arms.

'Here, many women are still not used to being in the company of men from outside their family. For them it is easier to be tended by women, even in emergencies. You will see in the hospital—in the general part of it, not the specialist centre— that we are bringing in more women doctors and all our nurses are also women, although more men are now seeing nursing as a possible career path.'

Arun's explanation was so clear—his mind so obviously focussed on medicine—she felt ashamed of her reaction to that smile.

The ambulance slowed and the doors opened, and Mel experienced the familiar rush of an ambulance arrival at a major hospital. It was the same all over the world, except that here, as Arun stepped out to take the baby while Mel alighted and Tia was wheeled out, men and women bowed their heads, some murmuring words of respect.

'They forget this when I'm on the ward,' he said to Mel as she reached out to take the baby from him. 'There I'm treated with as much or as little respect as I happen to earn that particular day.'

She had to smile, although her anxiety for the tiny scrap of humanity in her arms was growing. His lips and tiny fingernails were now a deep blue, and his little heart raced so hard she could feel it thudding against his ribs.

Arun must have seen the anxious glance.

'X-ray first, then what?' he asked, as he led the way through a pristine A and E department and along a passageway, following the trolley with Tia on it. 'An echo? Intubation?'

'We need oxygen to blow across his face first to make sure he's maximising his oxygen intake. Then fluoroscopy to look at his heart,' Mel suggested. 'You have all the machines—CT scanners, MRI's?'

'All mod cons,' Arun remarked and Mel heard a tinge of bitterness and wondered just how hard his job must be, attempting to change the hospital from one of private, and probably exclusive, specialisation to a place where all the people of his country could and would be treated.

A caring man! This facet of his character

shouldn't surprise her, but it did, making her realise how little she really knew of him.

Mel glanced his way as he spoke to a woman hovering beside them, studying the strong features, hearing authority in his voice, although he spoke quietly. The woman disappeared, then returned, wheeling a crib. It had an oxygen bottle attached and Mel turned her full attention back to the infant, putting the tiny boy into the crib and adjusting the flow of oxygen so it blew across his face.

The woman moved to push the crib but Mel gently eased her aside.

'I'll take him,' she said, anxious to keep watch on him at all times.

They went up in a lift then out into a wide corridor, where Tia was wheeled into a large private room and transferred to the bed.

'Would she like to hold the baby while we organise things—or you organise things?' Mel suggested.

Arun took the baby's crib over close to the bed and spoke to Tia, who shook her head violently and let fly another barrage of words, these sounding harsh and guttural.

'She doesn't want to hold him because then she will love him and if he dies, if we kill him with what we are doing, she will be heartbroken.'

The stark statement made Mel pause and she looked up to see the sudden fear she was feeling mirrored in Arun's eyes.

'We *could* kill him,' she murmured helplessly. 'Babies do die in our attempts to save them.'

Arun nodded, then said, 'But if it was your baby, would you not at least try to save him?'

Mel's hand went automatically to her stomach, the protective gesture not lost on Arun.

'I don't know how you can continue to do this work,' he said quietly, and she shook her head, understanding that he thought her fear was for the baby when in reality it was far more selfish— a totally irrational fear for herself. Although that was wrong—it wasn't for herself but for the baby, in that he or she would be motherless if…

CHAPTER FOUR

MEL blocked it all from her mind.

'The tests—we need to start at once,' she reminded him. 'Where do we go?'

He nodded agreement and led her from the room, but the quick glance he'd shot her told her he knew she'd ignored his statement.

And that the conversation wasn't finished.

The radiology department was as up to date as Jenny had said it would be, and technicians, no doubt alerted by Arun, were on standby. Mel explained the views she'd need, and left the baby with the radiologist while she and Arun studied the pictures on the screen.

'His heart's enlarged,' Arun said, using his pen

to outline it. 'But it's hard to see clearly. We need an echo?'

'Just a minute,' Mel said, watching the image change. 'See there.'

She took Arun's pen and pointed. 'It's blurry but it seems to me there's only one blood vessel coming out of the heart.'

'Truncus arteriosus?' Arun's voice was grave. 'We should fly him out.'

'To where? How far does he have to go to a specialist centre with a heart bypass machine? Because he'll need open-heart surgery, Arun, and need it soon—and I have concerns about flying so fragile a baby anywhere.'

'Can you be sure that's what it is?'

He wasn't doubting her, Mel knew, just reminding her there were more tests available.

'No, but we'll do an echo, that should tell us, and just to make sure, an MRI scan. They're all non-invasive and can be done quickly. I could do a cardiac catheterization, which would show the extent of the malformation, but I'd rather not put him through that if we don't have to.'

Arun spoke to the technician who wheeled an echocardiogram machine close to the crib and rubbed gel on the baby's chest. Once again Mel and Arun watched the monitor, although they would get all the results printed out and would be able to study and compare them later.

'See,' Mel said, again using the pen. 'One thick artery coming out of the heart and, here, a hole between the two ventricles.'

'We have a heart bypass machine.'

His voice was strained, as if the words had been forced out of him against his will.

And Mel understood why. He was a proud man, brought up in the ruling family of his country. To ask a favour of someone would be very, very hard.

And, she guessed, asking a favour of a woman would be even harder.

She turned her attention from the screen to his face, wiped clean of any emotion, although his eyes told of his stress.

'You want me to do it?'

'You're very good, I've heard enough of you

to know that, seen DVDs of your work. And your ambition has always been to have your own paediatric surgical unit, to be the head of one with all the best equipment money can buy so babies from your regional hospital don't have to be sent to other places. If you are willing to do this for us, whether the baby lives or dies, I will guarantee you the equipment you need to achieve that ambition.'

Mel stared at him in disbelief.

'You're bribing me? You're bribing me to do an operation to save a baby's life?'

She wasn't sure if the radiologist and technician understood English, but she was so angry she didn't care.

'How could you think so little of me that you'd offer me money? It's a baby's life we're talking about here, not some pathetic tummy tuck!'

Arun held up his hands in surrender.

'It is asking too much of you—you're a visitor in our country, a guest. It is not your problem.'

He was losing ground with every word, but his pride and his upbringing made the situation impossible. He was a giver of favours, not one who asked for them, and this woman had already thrown him off balance once today.

Badly off balance…

He fought back the memory of her revelation and concentrated on what she was saying.

'Forget asking too much of me, and start thinking of how to get what we'll need. Two weeks after birth is the optimal time for a truncus arteriosus repair because if we leave it longer than that the increased pressure on the pulmonary arteries and other pulmonary vessels can cause irreversible damage. What we need to do is get him as strong and stable as we can in that time…'

'You can stay that long?'

He realised as soon as he'd asked the question that it had been stupid. Surely, given the circumstances of her pregnancy, she must have arranged to stay at least that long so they could discuss the future of their child. Or had she intended telling him then departing as soon as possible?

'I can stay.'

Her eyes defied him to question that statement but once again his mind seemed to have divided, one part concentrated on Tia's baby and the operation he would require, the other on the unbelievability of what was happening here. First the woman he'd thought never to see again reappearing in his life.

Carrying his child!

No, he couldn't afford to think about that right now.

But add the fact that she was the one person this baby needed to save his life, and here she was, right on hand to do the operation.

It *had* to be fate.

He followed the practical part of his mind, locking down the fate-flustered one in a distant corner.

'So what will you need?'

'*We* will need either a very small donated human artery with an intact valve for a homograft or a very small dacron artery with a manufactured valve.' She emphasised the 'we' just enough to let him know he was going to be taking equal responsibility for this operation. 'A donated human artery is best if you can get one small enough because it has the ability to develop normally so might reduce the need for further operations as he grows.'

'Kam and I, working with our own staff, have been cryo-preserving donated tissues for more than a year now. I'm sure we'd have what you need. And what about the patch for the hole between the left and right ventricles?'

'I should be able to use a piece of the pericardial sac, which will save any rejection problems, otherwise we can fix it with…'

She paused, and studied Arun's face, although he doubted she was seeing it, simply using it as a focus as she thought ahead.

'Sometimes we leave it open for a while in case the new artery causes high ventricular pressure but, no, I think we should close it if we can.'

'And for now?'

'Ah!'

Melissa looked down at the tiny baby in the

crib. He would need to be as strong as possible before the operation, so optimal oxygen intake, some medication to help the heart work more efficiently and not over-strain, and adequate nutrition through high-calorie formula or breast-milk, possibly with supplemental feedings.

'Would Tia nurse him?' Mel quietly asked Arun, remembering how the young woman had reacted to being asked to hold the baby.

Arun looked from Mel to Tia then back to Mel.

'I doubt it, but I could ask.'

Mel shook her head.

'Let's not upset her any more, but maybe if we can arrange to care for the baby here in her room, she might grow interested enough to want to hold him.'

Arun nodded, then *he* shook his head.

'You are one amazing woman,' he said, startling Mel because he sounded as if he really meant it and *that* made her feel all warm and fuzzy inside.

Dangerous stuff, warm and fuzzy!

'I'm not doing any more than anyone would,'

she told him, hoping she sounded practical enough to hide her reaction. 'We can put in a nasogastric tube to feed him, which will save him using what little energy he has sucking either a breast or a bottle, and I need an IV line and an oximeter to keep an eye on the oxygenation of his blood and…'

She paused, wondering what else the fragile infant would need.

'And?' Arun prompted.

Mel shook her head.

'I want to keep things as minimally invasive as possible to give him every chance to get stronger. From a purely cardiac point of view, what do you think?'

'Let's get someone in to watch him so we can sit down somewhere quiet and work out a plan, looking at what we hope to achieve before the operation and what negatives might make it impossible to leave it for two weeks.'

He didn't wait for her answer but disappeared out the door, leaving Mel with the baby, and his mother, who lay with her face turned to the wall.

Having assured herself the baby was managing as well as could be expected, Mel crossed to sit beside the new mother.

'This is so hard for you—I can understand that—but I'm nearly sure we can fix what's wrong with him. Had you chosen a name?'

Dark eyes opened and were soon awash with tears.

'I cannot give him the name,' Tia whispered. 'It is the name my husband chose, and if the baby dies he will want it for the next baby.'

'Oh, love,' Mel said, putting her arm around the young woman's shoulders, overwhelmed by the sadness in Tia's voice. 'This isn't your fault, you know. Babies are often born not quite right. No one is to blame.'

Seeing this comfort wasn't working, Mel tried another tack.

'Where *is* your husband? Are husbands not allowed to be present at the baby's birth in your culture? Is that why he's not here?'

The dark hair moved from side to side then Tia raised her head again.

'He's in America. He's studying. His father said he had to stay there—that he couldn't come home just to be with me for the baby's birth. I should have gone with him and been there and had the baby in an American hospital, but when I went to America before, I was so homesick I said I wouldn't go.'

Mel gave her a comforting pat.

'Where you had the baby wouldn't have made any difference,' she explained. 'This is something that happens when you are very newly pregnant, maybe eight weeks or so—the little heart just doesn't develop properly. But I have operated on babies as small as yours to fix their hearts, and they have been perfectly all right later.'

This time Tia turned right around and even hitched herself up on her pillows.

'You have? You can operate on tiny babies and fix their hearts?'

Hope crept cautiously into the words and flickered in the dark, tear-washed eyes.

'I have, and I can,' Mel told her, stroking Tia's long hair back from her face and smiling gently at the young woman.

'And you can fix my baby?'

Arun, returning to the room with one of his most trusted nurses, saw the improvement in his sister then heard the question and read Melissa's dilemma in her hesitation.

Would she lie?

He rather doubted it but for a moment he wished she would, just to keep Tia from diving back into the depths of misery.

'I cannot promise that, but more than ninety per cent of babies we operate on for this condition do survive. In fact, they not only survive, they thrive. It will take a little time, he'll need to be specially cared for before and after the operation, just for a few days, then another week in hospital. Later on, there are infections he might be susceptible to, and as he grows he might need another operation, but there's no reason he won't do well.'

Arun remained where he was, his arm held out to prevent Zaffra from entering the room. Melissa seemed to have worked some kind of miracle in getting Tia interested in the baby, and he didn't want to interrupt until he was sure the conversation was finished.

'I heard Arun say you must talk about what you have to do. Can I hold him—the baby—while you talk?'

Arun felt a grin as wide as the desert split his face and saw similar delight in the way Melissa hugged Tia.

'Of course you can. I'll put him in your arms then fix the oxygen so it blows across his face. That way most of what he breathes is pure oxygen, which will ease the workload on his heart.'

She crossed the room and gently wrapped the swaddling cloth around the infant then lifted him from his warmed mattress, carrying him across to his mother, who would warm him with her body.

'You take your time to look at him,' she told Tia. 'Later we'll put a feeding tube into his nose and he'll have to wear a nappy so we can work out how much fluid he's losing, but for now just hold him and marvel at the miracle a new baby is.'

Arun brought Zaffra forward and introduced

her to both women then, while Melissa placed the oxygen tube from the wall unit so it would blow across the baby's face, Arun watched Tia's bemusement as she examined her little son.

'But he looks perfect,' she said, after checking all the limbs and digits were in place. 'Except his little feet are blue and his fingernails and lips.'

And Arun was pleased to see she was right. The baby had finally achieved some pinkness in the rest of his body so the oxygen was working.

'Later,' he told his sister, 'when Melissa and I have talked, I will sit down and explain what is wrong and how we fix it. I will draw you a picture so you understand and can show Sharif when he comes home.'

Tia nodded and, satisfied his sister was now as comforted as it was possible to be with a very sick baby on her hands, Arun touched Melissa on the shoulder and indicated they should leave.

'We won't be long,' she promised, turning back as she reached the door to reassure Tia once again.

Tia smiled as if confident Melissa meant exactly what she'd said.

'Working miracles with mothers now, are you?' he asked Melissa as he led the way down the corridor to his suite of rooms.

'It's hard for them,' was all the reply he got, and he turned back to see that, far from looking happy at what she'd achieved, Melissa looked… depressed?

Sad, anyway. Sad enough for him to want to put his arms around her, draw her close and hold her until the sadness went away.

Hold her?

Madness lay that way!

But sadness?

'Is it worse than you've been saying, the baby's heart?' It was a guess, and he knew it was the wrong one when she shook her head.

'No, it's the grief,' she said, studying his face as if hoping to see understanding there.

But how could she when he didn't understand what she meant?

'Grief?'

'Think about it, Arun,' she continued. 'A woman goes into labour, goes through childbirth, and though it's messy and painful at least there's joy at the end—a healthy baby to hold and cherish. For Tia, and mothers like her, where the outcome's not as good, she has to suffer the loss of that healthy baby she was expecting—she has to grieve for it. And while grieving, it is hard to accept the other baby—the one she did have—the one that's fragile and in need of care she has to rely on strangers to provide.'

He stared at her, then shook his head.

'I can't believe I've never thought of it that way,' he murmured, awed by the depth of her understanding and feeling something for this woman that went beyond renewed attraction.

This pregnant woman, he reminded himself as she let him off the hook with a smile.

'Your heart patients are usually a whole lot older and often victims of their own over-indulgence, so you see heart problems from a different perspective.'

He nodded acceptance of her excuse, but now his brain had thrown up the fact of her pregnancy once again and the knowledge that it was his baby she carried hit him like a shock from a faulty electrical connection.

His *baby*—she was carrying *his* baby!

OK, he could just about accept that, but how he felt about it—that was the problem. Would his thoughts become clearer as his mind reached full acceptance?

Would it have been easier to think about it if Tia's baby hadn't arrived so inopportunely?

What he did know was that this was hardly the time to be working out what he felt, let alone what he intended doing about it…

'So, a plan,' Melissa said, as Arun resumed their walk towards his office, finally opening a door and waving her into a large room, furnished with a wide desk littered with papers, and a leather-clad lounge suite set around a coffee-table.

A coffee-pot, cups and trays with a selection of cakes and fruit had been set out on the table.

'I thought you might need a snack,' he said, leading her towards one of the comfortable-looking chairs. 'It is terrible that we have whisked you from the stables to the hospital with no time for you to relax, to bathe and change, or even to eat something. So sit, eat, and then we'll talk. I had coffee sent up but if you'd prefer tea or a cold drink of some kind…'

Mel shook her head, although now she was away from the baby and had relaxed slightly, she realised she was starving.

'Coffee's fine, but with a lot of milk, if you have it,' she said, sliding into the big armchair and leaning forward to examine the enticing-looking pastries on display. 'And these are?'

'Various sweet treats, mostly flavoured with rose or orange syrup and honey, but also with nuts sprinkled between the layers of pastry. You will find similar pastries right across the Middle East, all the way through to Greece in Europe and Morocco in North Africa.'

Mel chose a pastry and bit into it, feeling the sweetness fill her mouth then honey dribble from her lips.

Arun came closer, a serviette in his hand, but rather than hand it to her he caught the tiny drop of honey on it, his fingers brushing the soft paper of the napkin across her lips at the same time. His body bent over her, his face close enough for her to see the stubble of beard and the shadow of tiredness beneath his eyes—lines of strain that had not been there when they'd met four months ago.

The time had not been kind to him and she felt a surge of sympathy. If health care in his country was as neglected as Jenny said, he must have enormous worries on his shoulders.

But he was also close enough for her to see, as he bent towards her, desire leaping in his eyes, a desire that was echoed in her body.

Her nipples peaked and her breasts swelled as anticipation tingled through her body.

Would he kiss her again?

Would she respond?

Wouldn't kissing Arun just make things more complicated?

Then, with his lips close enough to kiss if she straightened just a little, he moved away, leaving her feeling a sudden sense of loss.

Stupid! Irrational! How could she even think of kisses at a time like this?

'Arun?'

His name escaped in a sigh so soft Arun was sure she hadn't meant to say it but he responded anyway, bending over her again to brush the honey-tasting lips with his. To brush her name, 'Melissa', on them.

The chemistry that had worked between them from their first meeting flared back to life. Arun's hand slid around the back of her head, his fingers weaving into her hair, holding her captive.

Or was it *her* clasp on *his* head that held them together?

The kiss deepened, Arun feeling the power of it as desire shuddered through his body, tightening his muscles and heating his blood.

This was madness.

The baby…

They should stop…

She broke away from the kiss but not before he'd felt enough of her response to know the chemistry still worked for her as well. Now, leaning back in her chair, defiance shaded the desire he knew he'd read in her eyes.

'We have to talk about the baby,' she said. 'About Tia's baby.'

'And your baby? The one you say is mine? When will we talk of it?'

'The one I *say* is yours?'

Her disbelief was like another person in the room yet, now the words were out, he realised he did have doubts. With reason, for how could he be sure?

'How do I know you didn't take another lover immediately after me? Or have one before me, close enough that you can pass off the child you carry as mine?'

He spoke coldly, the words damning her, but surely he was right to be suspicious. Her reaction was immediate—the fire of anger in her eyes and fury in every line of her body as she rose to her feet and glared across the table at him.

'My love life is not, and never has been—apart from ten short days—any of your business, but

I can assure you the baby is yours.' She spat the words at him, as angry as a maltreated cat—her hands clenched, perhaps to stop her clawing him as well as mauling him with words. 'Now it's up to you. I will pretend you didn't say what you just said to me and we sit down and discuss the baby's problems—Tia's baby's problems—and together work out a treatment plan, or you call your pilot and get the plane ready to fly him out.'

She was right—Tia's baby was the issue. How could he have been so easily diverted?

Because he'd kissed her?

Tasted honey on her lips?

Felt the frantic beat of need in both their bodies?

Or because he was beginning to accept that what she'd said was true—that she carried his child? Added to which was the fact that, while in theory marrying and having a child was all very well, in reality the thought of fatherhood was very unsettling. What did he know about raising a child? Could he, who'd barely known his father, be a good father to a child?

He nodded stiffly, waited until she seated herself

again, then sat opposite her, outwardly calm—he hoped—but inwardly churning with such a tumult of emotions he couldn't put names to them.

Mel watched him settle back in his chair. She took a deep breath, trying to calm her thudding heart, to settle the fear and hurt she felt inside.

But she hadn't got to where she was, a top paediatric heart surgeon, without being able to hide her emotions successfully. She hid them now and matched his earlier coldness with her own.

'So, shall we discuss this case?'

He hesitated long enough for her to realise few people gave him orders, but in the end he nodded.

And scowled at her.

Ignoring the scowl, she leant forward, opened the file and spread the prints on the table.

'You can see here the artery leaves the ventricles as one big trunk, and here, the hole in the ventricular wall. The problem is that too much blood is flowing through the pulmonary arteries where they branch here…' she pointed with a pen that had been beside the file on the table

'…into the lungs, causing congestive heart failure. From the look of this there's a narrowing of the aortic arch as well, so the heart is having to work extra hard to get blood flowing around the rest of the body.'

'And the operation?'

She glanced up at the interruption, pleased he had switched his attention from personal matters, feeling her own inner agitation ease as they spoke professionally.

'I need to detach the pulmonary artery from the main artery and use a small piece of artery with valves intact to connect it the right ventricle, stitch it in place there, fix the hole between the ventricles and patch up the aorta where I've detached the pulmonary artery.'

'That's a huge operation for so young a child,' he said, frowning over the scans, following the lines she'd drawn with the pen. 'Saying it like that, you make it sound simple, but for an infant…'

He lifted his head to look at her, and Mel read the doubt in his eyes—doubt and pain.

'There's a ninety per cent success rate,' she

said, to quell the doubt. The pain was something else. 'She means a lot to you, Tia?'

This time he looked surprised, then he offered Mel a twisted kind of smile, so sad it nearly broke her heart.

'Tia's mother, Miriam, was my father's favourite wife. She was also more a mother to Kam and me than our own mother was. Tia was an afterthought, the last child of my father, and Kam and I, when we came home from school in England, regarded her as our special pet—a living doll, I suppose, although boys are not meant to play with dolls.'

'Boys can play with anything they like,' Mel replied gently, hearing the pain and loneliness of the child he'd been behind the simple explanation. 'And this boy will, too, because we're going to fix his heart,' she added, to get them back on track. Feeling sorry for this man was a sure way to disaster. She was already doomed to feel attraction—but sympathy? Empathy?

Way too dangerous!

'For now we need to keep an eye on his oxygen

saturation. Because of the hole in the ventricular wall, the oxygen-rich blood from his lungs is
mixing with the oxygen-depleted blood from his
body, which means the blood going into the aorta
isn't as oxygen-rich as it should be.'

She glanced across at him and smiled.

'Teaching my grandmother to suck eggs, aren't
I?' she said.

'Your grandmother to what?'

'It's an old expression—telling you things you
already know.'

He returned her smile—with interest apparently because it made her forget all the reasons
she didn't want to be attracted to Arun again.

Although, now he knew about the pregnancy…

Was she mad?

Of course they couldn't continue their affair.
It would complicate matters far too much.

And, no doubt, start the dreams again—
dreams where he held her in his arms, and
brought such sensual joy to her body…

'I thought we were sensibly discussing the

baby's case,' he said quietly, and she looked across at him and saw a smirk that suggested he'd read her momentary distraction with ease.

'We are!' she protested, but it was a feeble effort. Somehow she had to shut away all memory of the past and concentrate on the present—now. 'I was saying how I needn't explain it all to you.'

'Ah, but you do, because although I know what is wrong and what must happen, hearing you explain will help me tell Tia.'

Mel understood and continued to run through the regimen the baby would need, with tube feedings for maximum nutrition, ACE inhibitors to dilate the blood vessels and make it easier for the heart to pump blood through the body, digoxin to strengthen the heart muscle, diuretics to help the kidneys remove excess fluid.

'So, we organise all of this now, and have nurses rostered on to keep an eye on him at all times,' Arun said. 'What about a doctor? Do you want a registrar to keep an eye on him? We could fly in a paediatric registrar.'

'You could? From where? Do you pluck them out of the air?'

She was teasing him, Arun knew, and for a moment he wondered if they could get back to where they'd been, not necessarily lovers again but two adults enjoying each other's company, talking and laughing easily, discussing every subject under the sun.

Except the future, which had been off limits, for they'd agreed that what they'd both wanted had been a brief affair. And if, in retrospect, it had seemed much more than that...

He forced his mind back to practicalities, at the same time registering that very soon the future would *have* to be discussed.

The baby's future—*his* baby's future...

'As I said, Kam and I have been working on changes at the hospital. The maternity ward came first, but paediatrics was to come next. We have been interviewing applicants for the positions available—a paediatrician and three paediatric registrars—and I am sure at least one of those we've short-listed could come immediately.'

'That would be great.' She sounded genuinely pleased so he wouldn't mention that money might have to change hands to achieve this as quickly as possible. Mention of money—or of what money could provide for her—had upset her earlier, despite his experience of women suggesting they were far more practical about gifts or payments for services than men were.

But this woman was unlike any woman he'd ever known—the dreams that had cursed his nights for the past four months had been enough to tell him that. And though, whenever he'd considered following up on their brief affair—maybe flying to Australia to see her—he'd ruthlessly dismissed the thought as a passing fancy, he'd known the attraction went deep.

Now she was here.

Carrying his child...

And about as friendly as a hungry barracuda!

'I will get moving on the medications first. You will fit the feeding tube? Should he be sedated for that?'

'A mild sedative.' She picked up a pen and

turned over one of the printouts to write a list of what she'd need on the back of it, but as she pushed it across the table to him, their fingers touched. She drew her hand back as though she'd been burned and Arun knew she'd felt the searing awareness that had shot through his own blood at the touch.

'No,' she said, answering a question he hadn't asked. 'Later, when we have this baby stable, that's when we'll talk.'

He took the list and guided her back to Tia's room, leaving her there with the two women and the baby while he went to organise first the equipment and drugs and then another doctor so Melissa wouldn't have to spend all her time at the hospital.

Although he suspected she was conscientious enough to want to be here a lot of the time.

Which meant that, apart from the promised talk, he'd see precious little of her, as all her spare time would, naturally, be spent with Jenny, preparing for the wedding, doing girl things...

By the time he returned to Tia's room, it was

filled with relatives. At least the hospital had been built with local customs in mind so the rooms were big enough for a mass of family to squeeze in, but to intubate a fragile baby with such chaos all around?

'I know I said it would be good for the baby to stay with Tia,' Melissa said, when he'd battled through the crowds to the side of the crib where she was fending off women who wanted to hold the newborn, 'but this is impossible, and he really needs to be monitored. An ICU room perhaps, but one somewhere not too far away so Tia can visit and sit with him, just her and maybe Miriam, not the whole family.'

'It will be hard to explain that to them,' Arun said, 'but, yes, you're right. We need to move him. Come.'

He handed the equipment he'd brought with him to Zaffra and pushed the crib from the room, calling back to Tia that he would come back and see her very soon.

CHAPTER FIVE

'Is IT always like that in your hospital?' Mel asked, as she once again followed Arun along a wide corridor.

'The family thing?' he asked, glancing back over his shoulder and smiling at her. 'Pretty much. It's harder to handle at night when the lights are dimmed because family members tend to sleep on the floor of the hospital room and you can trip over them if you're not careful.'

They reached a double door, which Arun pushed open with one shoulder, and Mel followed him into a very modern ICU, the nurses at the central desk watching monitors, while other nurses could be seen through the windows that gave clear views into the patient rooms.

'This first room is empty and there's a procedure room beside it. We'll take him in there first to fit the feeding tube and a port for drugs, then hook him up to the monitors in the room.'

He led her into a small but well-equipped procedure room, then, to Mel's surprise, he swept off his shirt then stripped off his jeans.

'I should have changed earlier but there didn't seem to be time,' he said, no doubt reading surprise in her eyes.

But he'd read wrongly this time, for she was mesmerised not by him changing clothes but by the sight of his strongly muscled chest, his skin gleaming with good health, dark against the stark white underwear he wore.

Mesmerised by memories…

The desire she'd battled to keep at bay since first they'd met again erupted in her body, and it was only as he turned towards the sink to scrub that she remembered where she was, and what she was supposed to be doing.

She crossed the room to scrub beside him, then realised she, too, must smell of horse. He'd pulled a scrub suit from a cupboard by the sink—there'd be another one there. But though at times throughout her training she'd often shared a changing room with men, she was suddenly shy at the thought of disrobing in front of Arun.

Maybe he wouldn't look…

If she did it quickly…

Was she mad? There was a baby here in need of help—*that* was the issue, not her, or Arun, or modesty, or anything else.

She found a scrub suit, stripped off her loose tunic and trousers and pulled on the suit before joining him at the sink, using the foot pedal to get water, scrubbing her hands and arms, the motions automatic as she'd done it so often before.

'Have you been well in your pregnancy?' he asked, and Mel turned to stare at her companion. It seemed the most unlikely of questions, but she could read no hidden message on his face.

'Fighting fit,' she told him, rinsing off the soap and bumping the hot air dryer with her shoulder to set it going.

He was pulling on a glove from the dispenser on the wall, taking two from the box next to it—mediums—and handing them to her.

'That's good,' he said, and once again Mel searched his face, certain this weird conversation must have a hidden agenda.

But all she saw was the strong-planed features that had first attracted her, the slightly hooked nose that had suggested arrogance though he'd never directed it at her, the unusual green eyes, pale and beautiful, and the lush lips whose magical powers had driven her body to distraction.

She crossed back to tend the baby, looking first at what Zaffra had laid out on the treatment table, taking the baby's chart to check his weight so she could calibrate the strength of the drugs she would give him, measuring him so she knew how long to make his feeding tube, thinking all the time of the problems that could arise and how to circumvent them if she could.

They worked well together, Arun decided as he held the sedated baby while Melissa inserted the feeding tube and taped it into place. She'd already slid a cannula into a vein on the back of one tiny hand and taped it into place, splinting the little arm so the access port couldn't be accidentally dislodged.

Now, as Zaffra settled him back on the warmed mattress of the crib, Melissa bent over the table, writing furiously, doing sums and checking them, working out dosages and feeding formulas, Arun guessed, although she was too absorbed in her work to explain.

So absorbed she probably didn't realise she was chewing slightly on her bottom lip as she worked.

He'd chewed gently on that lip, he remembered. It had been late one night, and they'd attended lectures during the day but had skipped the formal dinner, going off instead to a little waterside restaurant he'd heard was good. They'd walked back along the beach towards the hotel, rounding an outcrop of rocks and coming to a smaller cove, so deserted, so enticing, they'd stripped off and swum.

That had been when he'd nibbled on her lip.

Nibbled on it as he'd held her close, making love in the water…

Making love in the water!

Unprotected!

He'd half remembered earlier—an instance of stupidity—but hadn't placed it until now. Although it hadn't seemed like stupidity at the time.

Madness perhaps, but not stupidity.

And now?

So the baby *could* be his and she *hadn't* told him!

For four months she hadn't told him.

He couldn't think about it right now, not with Melissa standing there, looking at him as if expecting some reply.

Had she asked a question?

About the baby?

It had to be.

'He's left us for another planet,' Mel said to Zaffra. 'So maybe you can tell me what formula you have in the maternity ward for newborn babies.'

'There are many—come and see,' Zaffra suggested.

Mel glanced at Arun, who was looking slightly less thunderous than he had a little earlier, though still angry enough to bite if teased.

'Will you hook him up to the monitors while I check out the formulas?' she asked.

He frowned at her so fiercely she wondered if it had sounded like an order instead of a request, but in the end he nodded abruptly then leant over the crib, moving it towards the wall where the monitors stood.

Two hours later they had the baby hooked up to monitors, nurses rostered to be with him at all times, feeding and medication regimens in place, and the little boy as safe and stable as they could make him.

'Come, I will take you back to Jenny's house,' Arun said, as Mel leant over the crib for the hundredth time, checking and rechecking, worrying and wondering. Had she done all she could? Would he be all right? Should she—?

'I don't know if I should leave him,' she responded worriedly. 'Not for any length of time. Jenny spoke of a party tonight—I should go to that, she'd be disappointed if I didn't, but to leave him now, just like that…'

Arun frowned at her

'You're tired—probably jet-lagged. You need to rest for a short time at least or you'll be little use to the baby.'

And as he said it, exhaustion hit her like a bus, her limbs suddenly too heavy to move. But she had to find the strength to argue.

'You're right, but what if the baby needs me? If something goes wrong?'

The look on Arun's face softened.

'You would not trust a cardiologist to watch over him?' he teased, and it must have been the tiredness that made her feel warmed and cherished by his tone. But then the meaning of his words sank in.

'*You'll* stay?' She stared at him and imagined she saw a shadow cross his face.

'You sound surprised,' he said, the coolness back in his voice suggesting the shadow had been hurt—a suggestion made fact when he continued. 'Do you think I care less for my nephew and my sister's peace of mind than you, a stranger, would?'

Mel shook her head and reached out to touch his scrub-suit-clad arm.

'I'm sorry. You're right. I *am* tired, also desperately in need of a bath and change of clothes and even some food if that's possible. Do you have on-call rooms where I can rest? Is there somewhere I can grab a sandwich?'

A stream of words she didn't understand greeted her questions, but the angry shaking of Arun's head told her it was probably just as well she didn't understand.

'On-call rooms? Grab a sandwich? Do you think we treat our guests so poorly?'

Then his voice softened and he smiled and lifted his hand to touch her cheek.

'Although we have treated you poorly, have we not, Melissa? Rushing you to the house to help the baby, bringing you here and feeding you nothing more than a pastry.'

Arun looked at her, at the wild red-gold curls escaping the theatre cap she'd pulled on earlier, at the pale, pale skin and grey-blue shadows beneath her eyes.

'At least I can offer you something more comfortable than an on-call room. Kam and I have an apartment on the top floor that we share from time to time, although it's rare both of us are there together. It's a convenience, you understand. I'll take you there, show you around, and by the time you are bathed, there will be food.'

'That sounds great,' she said, although the words were hesitant—the hesitation explained when she added, 'But won't that put you out? Wouldn't you want to use the apartment yourself?'

'I will stay near my sister and the baby,' he said, then couldn't help himself. 'So you will be perfectly safe.'

Bright colour rose beneath the pale skin.

'I'm sorry—I didn't mean it that way. I know you are an honourable man. It's...'

And he knew exactly what it was, because now, though both of them were tired and worried, the attraction that from the first had arced through the air between them was still alive and well, stirring, teasing, tantalising and tempting both of them.

He smiled, then leant forward and kissed her gently on the lips.

'There will be other times to finish that sentence. Other times for the talk you know we have to have, Melissa. But for now a bath, food and rest. Come.'

He led her along more corridors, then up in a lift, along another corridor and finally opened a door that led into a spacious living room, a wall of glass at the far side revealing the city spread out beneath them.

'Sit,' Arun commanded, and Mel was glad to obey. But he returned within minutes, held out his hand to help her to her feet, then led her to a bathroom where a rectangular tub was already half-filled with water. And floating on the top of the water, leaves—perhaps the source of the soft and subtle perfume that permeated the room.

'Towels, soap, lotions and a bathrobe.'

Arun waved his hand towards a white marble

bench where these and more were laid out. Bottles of every shape, beautifully coloured, like precious jewels, lined another, smaller ledge of marble higher up.

'New toothbrush, hairbrush. Anything you can't find, just press the button by the bath— and, no, it won't be me who comes to tend you but our maid.' He shot Mel a grin that would have done the devil proud. 'Your chaperone.'

And tired though she was, she had to smile back.

'If she lives here in this apartment, I'm sure she's well trained to notice nothing.'

'Maybe,' he said, but his smile had faded.

But no sooner had he shut the door than the conversation was forgotten. Mel stripped off the scrub suit and her undies, thinking she'd throw the lot away. Then, realising she might need the undies when she dressed again later, she soaked them in the washbasin, squirting hair shampoo in with them to make suds.

Then she turned off the taps and climbed into the bath, feeling the warm water envelop her weary body, feeling the tiredness leach from her skin as she relaxed back, her head against a slightly cush-ioned end. A bottle of bath gel was near to hand and she soaped herself all over, then relaxed again, letting the water wash the soap away.

Relaxed…

She'd been far too long! Had she fallen asleep? Fool that he was! He should made sure Olara stayed with Melissa while she bathed. But he'd sent Olara out to buy some clothes for their guest and Arun had assured her he could look after Melissa.

Did that include checking if she'd drowned in the bath?

He'd knock.

No answer.

He slid the door open, saying her name, softly at first and then more loudly, but she didn't hear, not because, as his first heart-stopping thought had been, she'd drowned, but because she was so deeply asleep.

And so nakedly beautiful his heart stopped again, though only for a moment, before speeding up, thudding with desire—terrible in a man who had guaranteed her sleep.

But as his gaze slid across her body, the shame he should and did feel turned to fascination. For there, protruding in a gentle curve, was her pregnant bump.

Water…

The ocean swim…

His baby?

'Melissa?'

This time he said it louder, kneeling by the bath, his hand under her chin lest she startle and slip beneath the water.

'Wake up, sleepyhead. If you need to rest, you'll be far more comfortable in bed.'

She turned her head towards him, the blue eyes puzzled at first, then, recognising him, she smiled.

'Arun,' she said softly. 'You're in my dream again.'

But the words were barely out when she sat up, sloshing water over him, moving so quickly he grabbed her slippery wet shoulder to steady her in case she slipped and fell back.

'Wait! Take it slowly. You've been asleep. Here!'

He wrapped her in a bath-sheet so her nudity wouldn't panic or embarrass her, and steadied her as she climbed from the deep bath, then he dried her carefully, working so his hands stayed always on the towel, not her skin, not wanting to startle her again.

And once dry he let her keep the towel while he lifted a white robe from the bench and slipped it over her head, helping her ease her arms through the sleeves then pulling the towel from underneath it so she stood, fully clothed, but no less desirable because the white silk was no softer than her skin, and the flaming hair stood out around her head like a beacon, drawing him towards her.

'I have set out some food by your bed, and a Thermos of tea should you want it—cool drinks as well, fruit juices and yoghurt. I will show you.'

He turned away from that beckoning beacon and led her into the bedroom, showing her the tray on wheels that held the food and folding back the bedclothes for her.

'I was famished before but now all I want to do is sleep. It must be jet-lag,' she said, turning from her survey of the room to face him. 'You'll wake me in time to see the baby before I have to leave for the party?'

'I'll make sure you're woken up,' he promised.

'Thank you.'

She said the words shyly, but maybe he was imagining it, and it was only tiredness muting her usually strong voice.

But he answered her in kind.

'It is my pleasure,' he said gently. 'Sleep well, and from the bottom of my heart I thank you. You have done my family great service today, Melissa. It will never be forgotten.'

Mel heard the words and wanted to protest—to say she'd done nothing more than any other person with her training would have—but she felt that might trivialise what Arun had just said, and it had sounded so beautiful she didn't want to do that.

So she smiled and, still smiling, carried his thanks to bed, where she curled her hands around her small bulge, patted it and spoke to it, apologising for being so neglectful in their communication today.

But as she spoke the ease the bath had given her and the joy of Arun's words faded, leaving room for worry about what the future held.

For her and her small bulge…

She woke up to a soft voice saying her name— 'Dr Miss'—it was close enough. Opening her eyes, she took in the young woman by the bed and slowly remembered the flight, the ride, the revelation—and then the newborn infant.

Jen, she'd barely spoken to Jenny. And where was Arun? How could she get back to the ICU to check the baby, then from the hospital to the compound where Jenny lived? Would she be in time for the party?

The young woman had disappeared. Had her job been to wake her up? Nothing more?

Too many questions that were impossible to answer so she lay for a while, thinking about fate, until hunger drove her from the bed. She washed and pulled on the satiny silk robe that matched the gown she wore, refusing to wonder why a bachelors' apartment would have such things at hand, then ventured forth.

The young woman was in the kitchen, looking anxiously at a bar laden with cut fruit and dishes of cold meat and cheese, small pancakes stacked on a silver platter and condiments in patterned jars and bottles.

'I do not know what you like to eat, but His Excellency said you would wake hungry and to feed you then show you the gowns.'

'I eat anything—but probably won't manage all of that,' Mel teased, hoping to take the anxiety from the soft, dark eyes.

She settled on a stool, picked up a pancake and wrapped some meat and cheese in it. The young woman offered her a jar.

'This is good, not too spicy.'

Mel dobbed a spoonful on her pancake, folded it over, and ate. Taste sensations she had never experienced before exploded in her mouth.

'It's delicious,' she said, and the young woman smiled and turned away, returning with a tall flask.

'It is tea,' she said. 'His Excellency said not coffee for you—not good for your baby.'

She smiled as she added the last phrase, saying, 'It is exciting, having a baby. So many babies, with my sister having one last week and Tia's and now you will have one. It is a sign the country will do well under the new sheikhs—a good omen.'

The woman was positively glowing with pleasure, and though Mel's main focus was on discovering all the various combinations of flavours of the food in front of her, a small part of it was wondering just how widespread the news of her pregnancy was. Jenny would be upset if she heard it secondhand and did this woman—had Arun mentioned her name?— know Arun was the father of her baby?

The pancake, her third, or maybe her fourth, lost its flavour and with a sigh she dropped it, half-finished, on her plate.

'I need to see the baby, but I have no clothes to put on. I'm sorry, I can't remember your name—'

'Olara,' the woman said, 'and there are gowns and underwear and other clothes for every day in the bedroom. His Excellency sent me to find things for you while you slept. You are going to the party—the wedding party tonight. He knew you would need something nice to wear. I will show you.'

The gowns were beautiful. Fine silk, decorated around the neck, on the sleeves and hem, with exquisite embroidery in gold and silver thread, they were so light it would be like wearing air.

Mel looked at them all, thinking choice would be impossible, finally settling on a dark blue, shot with purple. Purple was a little daring with red-gold hair, but tonight was special—Jenny's pre-wedding dinner—so daring should be OK.

Would she need a scarf?

She was wondering about this when she saw a row of hangers, each one holding a shawl to match a gown. Blue shot with purple on red-gold hair?

Olara hovered in the background—applauding her choice, producing a choice of new, still packaged, delicate underwear, showing Mel an array of make-up in a case as elaborate as a model's.

'I don't usually get dressed up like this,' Mel said, touching the soft silk of the knickers and the lacy confection that was a bra.

'But it is for the party,' the young woman told her. 'Everyone will be dressed up—I have a special dress as well.'

'You'll be going?'

Mel was sorry as soon as she'd said it, then hoped she didn't sound too surprised, but Olara seemed unbothered.

'Of course, we all go. We are the tribe, the family. You understand?'

'Not really, but I think it's wonderful that everyone can enjoy the party.'

She excused herself to shower, remembering as she towelled herself dry how gently Arun had dried her earlier—how circumspectly! Had she been less tired, she might have been disappointed that he hadn't touched her differently.

Oh, dear—what was she thinking?

In an attempt to block all thoughts of Arun—especially thoughts of him touching her—from her head, she dressed swiftly, pleased with the way the gown looked, even more pleased when Olara came back into the room and clapped her hands in delight, assuring Mel she looked very, very beautiful.

Searching through the make-up collection, she found a dusky mauve eye-shadow. Full war paint, she teased herself as she spread a skim of make-up on her face and added colour to her cheeks and eyes.

For Arun?

An enticement or a defence?

She couldn't answer either question, but as she pulled on the silver sandals Olara had produced, Mel decided it didn't matter. Tonight she was going to meet new people, learn new customs and have fun.

'You are beautiful!'

Arun was standing in the living room when she reached it, and his voice was so full of awe Mel knew he meant it. And suddenly she felt beautiful, although she knew, by and large, she was attractive at best, and that was mostly because of her colouring.

'Thank you,' she said, then to hide the delight his compliment had caused she added, 'You look pretty spiffy yourself!'

He was back in traditional dress, a white robe, although this one had rich and heavy gold decoration on the sleeves. The robes removed him from her—the remoteness she'd felt before—but at the same time they added another dimension to the attraction she felt towards him. She looked into his eyes, seeking the other Arun who was more familiar, and what she saw there made her mouth go dry.

Desire, so rampant she could feel it spreading from him through the air to touch her skin and through it to permeate deep into her body.

She *had* to resist, at least until they'd talked and sorted out the future of the baby—their baby.

Play it light.

She touched the gold.

'Special occasion robes?'

He smiled his agreement.

'Shall we go?'

He waved her towards the door and followed, and it wasn't until they were waiting for the lift that she remembered the other baby.

'Tia's baby—I must check him.'

She heard him sigh.

'I don't suppose my telling you I checked before I came up to collect you will make any difference.'

Mel shook her head, then remembered she was carrying her shawl over her arm. If she was going into the ICU she'd better put it on, although in such finery they were surely over-dressed for hospital visits. She lifted it to put it on, but Arun took it from her, draping it over her head, then crossing the two ends loosely under her chin before throwing them back over her shoulders.

'To cover that hair seems a sin,' he said, 'although many here would tell you not covering it is a worse sin.'

How could he speak when just his closeness

had dried her mouth again? How could he speak calmly when her body was so rattled by his proximity, and the intimacy of the action, she was surprised she was still upright?

Fortunately the lift arrived and they stepped inside then took the short journey down two floors to the ICU.

'How was he when you checked?' she asked, mainly to hide her reaction to his presence.

'Your charge is well. The monitors show his heart is not labouring too much, his kidneys are working without diuretics to help them, and Tia is badgering the nurses in an effort to get them to tell her more and more of what is happening and what the treatments mean. She has banished all the family except her mother, and has shifted into the ICU next to the baby.'

Arun smiled again.

'You worked a miracle in helping her accept the baby.'

'The miracle was the baby,' Mel said. 'Once she accepted that he might live, she was ready to fight both for him, and with him. She seems an intelligent young woman, so it will help her to know what is going on.'

Arun nodded, understanding and accepting what Melissa was telling him, but beneath the talk of the baby and Tia was his awareness of this woman.

The baby was indeed doing well, watched over by an exceedingly anxious-looking young woman, whose voice, when she spoke, suggested she was American. And if she was surprised to see a doctor in a flowing blue and purple robe and silver sandals entering the ICU room, she didn't show it, although Mel thought she read admiration in the younger woman's eyes.

But maybe that was for Arun…

'How do you do?' she said to Mel when Arun introduced her as Sarah Craig. 'I've read a paper of yours on the use of pericardial tissue for patches, and another on the pros and cons of not sealing the chest wound after open-heart surgery on very small children. Will you seal this one after the operation?'

Mel smiled at her, remembering the awe she'd felt—still felt—when she met people whose papers she'd admired.

Where had Arun magicked this woman from in the few hours while she had slept?

'You were working here in the hospital?' Mel asked Sarah, then turned to Arun for more information. 'You did have someone with paeds training already here?'

Sarah answered for him.

'I flew in an hour ago, and though I've been hoping to specialise in paediatrics, so far I've only got as far as spending a lot of time in kids' wards. The al'Kawalis interviewed me for a job here last week, and I was waiting to hear whether I'd been successful when Dr al'Kawali phoned me earlier today.'

Mel turned to Arun.

'No wonder the story of genies coming out of old lamps to grant wishes originated in this part of the world.'

He said nothing and though she wondered if money rather than rubbing a cloth on a lamp had produced the young doctor, Mel wasn't going to complain. She turned back to Sarah.

'As far as closing the chest, I won't decide that until we do the op,' she told her. 'In the meantime, it's our job to see this little lad is as strong as we can get him before we do it.'

'I think you'll find he's doing well,' Sarah told her, stepping back so Mel could examine the infant.

'That's his warrior blood,' she heard Arun's deep voice say behind her, but she was doing her best to ignore the owner of that deep voice so she didn't turn or falter in her examination.

'You're weighing him, and measuring his fluid input and output?' she asked, and Sarah handed her the chart.

'As I said, I've not long arrived, but the doctor who had been here gave me this.'

'It looks fine.'

Mel spoke easily, happy and relaxed now she'd seen the baby and knew he was doing as well as could be expected. She'd watch his weight gain and, if possible, do the operation before two weeks.

'As long as the heart muscle is strong enough—echoes should tell us.'

Sarah stared at her, a puzzled frown on her face, while behind her Arun was also looking a little bewildered—although she wasn't sure a face as strong as his could show such a feeble emotion.

'Sorry, thinking aloud—it's a bad habit. Usually there's just me and the baby and I'm telling him or her my thoughts. With a newborn, the heart muscle is weak and flabby, like a balloon full of water. I need that muscle firmer for a successful operation, that's why we have to feed him well and try to get him as strong as possible in as short a time as possible.'

She turned back to Arun, who was watching her with interest. Had he not expected her to be professional about this, considering her personal turmoil?

'Tia, is she about? Should I speak to her before we go?'

It was Sarah who answered.

'She's just gone to have a rest. She's not happy to be away from the baby for even the shortest

time, but the other lady—is it her mother?—
reminded her she needed her strength and took
her off to eat then sleep.'

'I'll see her later, then,' Mel said, and turned
to Arun. 'Shall we go?'

CHAPTER SIX

THEY walked out of the hospital through a wide entrance-way, decorated with so many lush plants it could have been a jungle.

'A jungle in a desert,' Mel murmured, noticing bright orchids flowering among the greenery.

'The magic of water,' Arun told her, 'and money, I suppose. Because the hospital was set up to attract wealthy clients, mostly from overseas, this foyer, their first view of the hospital, was designed to look as if they were entering a six-star hotel.'

'The familiarity of it making them relax,' Mel teased, but Arun wasn't smiling, and she guessed he was thinking of all that still needed to be done as far as medical services for his own people were concerned. 'Could you have done anything to change things before your father died?'

He sighed and shook his head.

'We did a little, here and there, encouraging doctors other than surgeons to come to work in our city, and we started on the modernisation of the old hospital, using our own money. No one in the government cared what we did there, but this was the place that had the equipment and the space to be a truly great hospital for our people as well as the foreigners.'

A long sleek black car had pulled up in front of them, and a porter from the hospital opened the back door.

Mel touched Arun's arm.

'Then you shouldn't have regrets—you shouldn't be looking back. You did what you could, and now you can do more. Holding onto the past adds to the burdens of the present, and you don't need that.'

He paused beside the open car door, turning to look at her—to study her—then he smiled, the kind of smile that made Mel's toes tingle and started a quivering hunger deep in her belly.

Had he felt a similar desire that he pressed a button, raising a darkened glass screen between the driver and the back seat?

But when he spoke she realised desire was the last thing on his mind.

'You must have some thoughts on your future with this baby,' he said, and Mel turned, hoping to see some glimpse of what he was feeling in his face.

No luck there—the word 'inscrutable' might have been coined for Arun's face right now. He had no need of veils or masks to hide his thoughts...

'I want the best possible upbringing for the baby,' she said, because, brain-boggled though she'd been, that was one thing she *had* decided. 'Maybe because I was brought up by a grandmother, I feel deeply that he or she should have two parents.'

Surely that would bring some twitch of emotion, some sign as to whether he was considering being part of the child's life. But, no—

not so much as a shift in a facial muscle, so Mel, feeling increasingly trapped and desperate, continued with a rush of words.

'That's not to say you have to be one of those parents. I mean, you can if you want—if you decide you'd like to be involved—and we can work out some kind of custody arrangement, but if you don't want to, well, that's OK, too. We— I mean, the baby and I—won't be alone as I have a good friend at home, Charlie, who has offered to marry me and be a good role model for the baby. I've said no to marriage and we haven't agreed anything, but I can tell you now that he loves kids and he's very well adjusted so he wouldn't have any hang-ups about it not being his biological child and—'

'Enough!'

She flinched not only at the harsh order but a thunderous expression on the previously blank face.

'What *is* this nonsense you are spouting? Who is this Charlie you intend to give my child to? Who knew about my child before I did? How—?'

He stopped as if his indignation was choking him.

Mel thought she'd start by answering the easy part.

'Charlie's an old friend. He's a great guy and has always been there for me. And I didn't tell him—he was worried about me and worked out for himself that I was pregnant.'

'Stop!'

Arun held up his hand this time.

'Strange as it may seem, I am not the slightest bit interested in the behaviour of this Charlie, although now he's entered the picture, how can you be sure it's my child you carry, not his?'

'Charlie's?'

Was it a measure of her tension that for a moment the question made no sense?

'But I've never been to bed with Charlie,' she managed. 'Charlie's a friend.'

'A friend, who, presumably, you *will* go to bed with once you've decided to marry him.'

Could frost form on words in warm desert climates?

Definitely!

But the coldest of frosts couldn't cool Mel's growing anger.

'I told you that I said no to marriage,' she began, but she doubted Arun was listening, for he'd given an explosive snort and was holding his head in his hands, with little regard for the neat points of his scarf.

'Can you tell me,' he demanded, in strangled tones, 'how this conversation got from my baby to making a life with this obviously bloodless man called Charlie? Although, before we leave him, why, if he so adores you, has he not taken you to bed? Is the man dead below the waist?'

Stung by this insult to her second-best friend, Mel rushed in again.

'Of course he's not—he's had dozens of affairs. Just not with me, because it wouldn't have been fair of me to have an affair with him knowing I didn't want to marry him. Besides, I've never wanted to have an affair with him— he's not that kind of friend.'

But blurting that out only made her feel more

confused and it obviously wasn't helping Arun for he was shaking his head in disbelief. He spoke into some kind of two-way radio and the driver slowed down slightly. Now Arun turned, put his hands on Mel's shoulders and peered intently into her face.

'You will listen to me,' he said, his voice deep and slightly raspy, as if it was only with difficulty he wasn't shouting at her. 'You will not marry Charlie. In fact, I do not ever want to hear his name again. It is bad enough that he knew of my child before I did, let alone that you would consider letting him take my place as the father. But there is one thing you got right in all that nonsense you have been spouting, and that's the fact that, ideally, a child should have two parents. You are one of those parents and I am the other, right?'

Where was this going?

Unable to guess, Mel did the only thing she could think of. She answered truthfully.

'Biologically speaking, yes,' she said, and saw the gold braid on Arun's gown catch the light from the bright lights outside the compound as he flung his arms into the air in sheer frustration.

'I am not talking about biological parents,' he growled. 'I had a biological father, thank you very much, and a lot of good he did me! My child will have a real father. Me!'

But how? Mel thought, although she thought it best not to say it. She'd upset him quite enough for one evening…

The building they stopped at, inside the compound, was yet another house, one Mel hadn't been inside before.

She glanced sideways at her companion, who'd been silent for the final minutes of the journey. What was he thinking? What did he mean about being a proper father to the baby?

The remote look on his face and his earlier anger suggested she'd be better off not asking.

Not right now…

'It's bigger than the others,' Mel said, as she got out and looked around, smelling the scent of lemon blossom on the warm night air.

'It was my father's house and though neither Kam nor I have any intention of moving into it, we will use it for functions and celebrations. Celebrations especially. It deserves some joy.'

He spoke calmly—tourist guide again—the anger gone.

Or hidden?

But hearing something in his words, Mel sighed. Just as she'd steeled herself against this forceful, sometimes overbearing man, he said something like that—the house deserving joy— and she caught a glimpse of an unhappy little boy inside him and started to feel sorry for him. Not that he'd accept sympathy from her—not this proud descendant of desert princes.

She adjusted the shawl around her head, knowing full well her rebellious hair would escape anyway, and followed him up the steps. He held her arm as she slipped off her sandals, and the touch fired again all the longings she'd been feeling.

Would it hurt to revisit the affair—to enjoy the pleasure they'd shared once before?

Of course it would, her brain shrieked, but her brain wasn't having a lot of control over her body right now, and she had doubts, if it came to an argument, as to whether her brain would win. Although going to bed with Arun wasn't going to help sort out the baby problem...

'This is the stateroom where visiting dignitaries from overseas are usually entertained.'

Arun led her into a room that looked like something out of an opera set. Colourful tapestries draped the walls, a long table seemed to be set with gold plate, though, when Mel looked more closely, she realised the plates were white and merely edged with gold. As were the glasses, and the vases that held displays of brilliant flowers, their colours merging with the colours of the coverings on the chairs, the curtains, the tapestries and the bright silks of the women.

'I understand why you men wear white,' Mel whispered, as they stood just inside the door so she could take in the scene in front of her. 'With all the other colours, you stand out.'

Arun smiled at her, then led her forward

towards one of the white-robed men. He saw them coming and stepped swiftly towards them.

'Brother,' he said, greeting Arun with a cheek-to-cheek embrace. Then he turned to Mel. 'And Melissa, best friend of my Jenny, who tells me you were put to work from the moment you got up this morning and that you are caring for our Tia's baby.'

He took Mel's hand and bent over it, then his fingers tightened on it as he looked into her eyes.

'The little boy? He is all right? Jenny said truncus arteriosus, but you can operate? Is that right? Can you spare us the time to do that?'

The green eyes, so like Arun's, looked worriedly into hers, but it was Arun who answered.

'Unhand the woman, Kam, and give her time to speak, although when she does she'll brush away your concern and assure you she wants nothing better to do than to hang around in Zaheer long enough to operate on Tia's baby.'

Kam laughed.

'I can see why you and Jenny are friends, Melissa. You think the same way. I tried to persuade Jenny we should take a honeymoon—at least a week away. Somewhere quiet we could be together, but could I get her to agree? Not when there is so much work to be done here, she tells me. She is going to be a slave-driver, that woman. This I know already.'

'You're talking about me?'

Mel turned to see Jenny, looking radiant in a gown of palest cream decorated with rich red embroidery. Her eyes gleamed with happiness and her skin shone with health, but it was the look she gave her husband-to-be that assured Mel her friend was really doing the right thing. These two were so in love you could warm your hands on the glowing warmth of it that shone in the air around them.

Mel glanced towards Arun, and knew he saw it, too, because although he smiled, his eyes looked sad.

He was thinking of his own wife, Mel guessed. A beautiful young woman who'd died too young, he'd said, though he'd not mentioned much more than the bare bones of the story.

'Hey, it's a party. Don't look sad.'

Jenny's teasing remark startled her out of her thoughts and she let her friend draw her further into the room where the Stapletons were standing talking to Miriam and another woman Jen introduced as the twins' mother.

More and more people, sisters by the dozen, nieces by the score, uncles, cousins, friends and family, everyone smiling but all the time checking out the strangers in their midst. But seeing Jen move among them, hearing her utter little phrases in their own tongue, Mel knew her friend would cope. In fact, this was probably the challenge Jen needed—not only marriage, but marriage that brought with it responsibilities she could handle—a marriage that would be a true partnership as she and Kam strove to bring their country into the twenty-first century.

But would the tasks in front of them make up for their lack of children? Would Jen's concern about not giving Kam an heir prove a tiny crack that could widen with time and spoil their bliss?

Don't even think about it, Mel's head warned,

but it was hard not to when she was carrying a child who could be the heir Kam and Jen needed.

The thought made Mel shiver as, for the first time, she considered her baby in that way. Originally, coming here, her mission—apart from being Jenny's bridesmaid—had been to tell Arun about the baby. And, aware from the beginning of their relationship that he hadn't wanted children, she'd thought the telling would be the beginning and the end of it.

But now?

Suppose he was serious about being involved with the child?

Worse still, suppose he saw her pregnancy as an option that saved him from marrying—an option he'd certainly not have chosen had Jenny not had the problem she had.

In which case he'd want the child brought up here, not in Australia, and how could she fight for custody against a man with seemingly limitless financial resources?

Jane was chattering about all she'd seen that day—the souk, the desert, the winter palace—

and Mel let the words wash over her, hoping they'd eventually chase away a new fear now nestling in her heart.

'You enjoyed it?'

They were in the limousine, returning to the hospital, when Arun asked the question.

'I did,' Mel said, telling him the truth, for the whole affair had been so mind-boggling she'd been able to set aside most of her anxiety about Arun's possible plans. 'The food, the conversation, everything—you certainly know how to throw a party.'

'Ah, but it's the people who make it happen,' Arun said. 'And family can be counted on to make things lively, can they not? They can fight and argue, yet remain friends. Kam and I, brought up mainly in schools overseas, have taken longer to learn this. But especially in the past, in the times when all the people roamed the desert, family had to come first to ensure survival. So it was always the most important thing, and though members of the family might squabble among themselves, in times of trouble they would stick together.'

Mel thought about his words—yes, there'd been arguments, some quite loud and fierce, at the dinner table, but there'd been laughter, too, and gentleness, a little girl sliding from her chair to walk around the long table and climb onto the knee of her white-robed father—the look of love in the man's eyes as he'd nestled the sleepy child on his lap wonderful to behold.

'I had a different kind of family to most,' Mel admitted. 'I was brought up by my grandmother, so my family was her, although in the holidays cousins came to stay.'

Arun touched her cheek, placing his hand against it so his palm curved under her chin.

'I could give you family,' he said, so quietly it took Mel a moment to process what he meant.

'You mean—'

'Marriage,' he said quietly.

Mel lifted her hand and rested it on top of Arun's.

'You can't mean that—you've barely had time

to think about all the repercussions of the baby. You'd be rushing into it, it's impossible—'

'You would consider marrying Charlie to give the baby a father, so why not marry me?'

'Charlie's safe.'

The words were out before she could stop them and no amount of 'oh, dear-ing' could take them back.

Yet Arun said nothing, his face closed against her once more, although she doubted it was the last she'd hear of the subject.

The car took them swiftly through the quiet night streets but not so swiftly that Mel missed the sight of the full moon riding high in the sky. The silvery beauty of it made her forget her concerns, her whole being caught up in the magic of the night.

'Oh, look at it,' she said. 'Could we stop where we stopped to watch the sunset so I can see the desert in the moonlight?'

Was he getting soft that such an innocent appeal could make his heart hurt? Arun wondered. Especially when he was angry with her?

'Charlie's safe'—what did that mean? That he, Arun, was dangerous?

But he gave an order to the driver and the vehicle turned off the main road, pulling up minutes later on the top of what had once been one of the highest sand dunes in the area.

Only now it had been stabilised and housing stretched down one side, while on the other side was the desert—the red-brown sands that still sang in his blood.

Perhaps that's why Melissa's words had affected him.

The driver opened his door but Arun told him to stay where he was, he would help the lady out. But the lady had already moved, opening the door and standing up, holding the door for support as she slipped off her sandals.

'You should keep them on. It's a lookout— there could be glass or rubbish lying about,' he told her, but she shrugged his words away.

'No worse than the needles that can be found on beaches at home,' she said, 'but I still love to feel the sand between my toes. The moon's bright, I'll walk carefully.'

And so saying she began to pick her way down the dune, the sand sliding with her in places so she had to hold out her arms to keep her balance. In the dark gown she looked like a shadow on the earth, but as he followed, the light wind lifted her shawl and he saw the flaming hair.

She was beautiful and he wanted her, not entirely, if he was honest, because of the baby. He wanted her physically, but he wanted more than that. The challenge of her, the meeting of their minds—she'd laugh if he said that.

He looked up at the moon and sighed, for it must be that which was making him so fanciful, but then she turned to face him, the moon shining on her face.

'It is beautiful,' she whispered. 'So beautiful I want to celebrate—to dance and sing out loud and, believe me, that's not a good thing because I'm a dreadful singer. But it awes me, if you know what I mean, yet makes me feel so good.'

Her obvious delight in the world that meant so

much to him filled him with a happiness he doubted he'd ever felt before. Very gently, he reached out and touched her, taking her face between the palms of his hands.

'I will show you all the desert,' he promised. 'By moonlight, and at sunset, and in the early dawn when it slowly wakens, pink and rosy like a woman, from a love-filled night.'

He leant forward and kissed her, long and deep, delving into her mouth, finding her tongue and tangling with it, drawing her breath into his lungs, sharing his with her, making promises with a kiss.

'If you will let me,' he added, moving so their bodies touched.

And through the layers of their clothing, through his robe and her gown, he felt her body respond, her nipples harden into tight nubs, even as his own desire became evident.

She kissed him back, leaning into him, her hands slipping beneath his scarf to hold his head to hers, then the kissing stopped and she slid her hand into his.

'Isn't this a bit public for a sheikh?' she whispered, the promise in the teasing words making his erection even harder.

It was too easy. They fell back into their special rhythm of love-making as if they'd never been parted. Mel felt her skin tighten in response to his touch, felt her body heat and soften for him. Felt the same heat in his skin, and in the bunching of his muscles as he lay beside her in the big bed—her big bed, not his—controlling his need until he had her almost begging to be taken.

'I have dreamt about this for four months,' he murmured into the sensitised hollow of her neck. 'I am not going to hurry.'

'Not until I beg?' she whispered, blurring the words against his short-cropped hair.

'I would never make you beg,' he promised, but as his fingers worked their magic she knew she might.

Soon…

Languor crept through her, so hot and heavy

she felt as if she was melting into the bed, yet all her nerve endings were alert, thrilling to the lightest brush of his fingertips or the briefest touch of his lips.

'Arun!'

She found herself whispering his name, pressing the word against the tight tendon of his shoulder.

'Melissa,' he murmured back, scything his teeth across her nipple so the next time she said his name it was gasped, not whispered.

So much sensation, her fingers reading his desire, her lips teasing him, while all the time the pressure built within them both, until Mel wondered who would give in first.

She did, for all his touch was gentle it was expert, while he watched her as if in wonder of the pleasure he could bring her, making her feel so special she floated on a sea of bliss, shattered only when the climax came, zinging first down to her toes then shuddering through her body, too dramatic to hide, too exhilarating to want to hide it.

Only then did he slide inside her, and once

again he teased, so the pleasure built and built again until they could peak together, shattering with cries they couldn't control, then lying, spent, in each other's arms.

Mel felt his weight against her and revelled in it, holding him close, hearing the sharp, deep intakes of the air he needed to replenish what he'd lost. She revelled in that, too. She hadn't had many lovers but she knew enough to know she pleased him, and that added to her own pleasure.

Then he was talking, but as she stopped thinking about pleasure and concentrated on his husky murmurs, she realised he was speaking in his own language, and from the way his hand pressed against her protruding belly, he was talking to the baby, not to her.

Oh, dear!

'Don't do that!' she pleaded, and she must have sounded anguished for he lifted his head to look at her, his hand pushing her wild hair back from her face so he could see her better in the moonlight.

'Don't talk to my child?'

He sounded more puzzled than affronted and she lifted her hand to press it against his lips.

'No, I didn't mean that—well, I did, but not that way. Nothing's decided. I know you mentioned marriage, but that's not a solution, you must see that. Your brother's married someone from outside your culture, and if you're marrying for children—to provide an heir—then surely you should marry one of your own people. Wouldn't that make it easier for him—the heir—to take over later? Make it easier for him to rule?'

She sighed and rolled away from him.

'I'm probably not making sense but I was in a muddle about this before you mentioned marriage, so imagine how much worse that muddle is now.'

'Why?'

Why?

She peered at him, searching for a valid reason, aware of the excited beating of her heart—but that was just, she was certain, because they were so good together in bed.

'Because it's silly even thinking of it.'

'Is it?'

He slid up in the bed and propped his hand on his elbow so he could look down into her face.

'I have promised Jenny and Kam I will marry and have children. I was happy to arrange a marriage of convenience. I already had Miriam looking for a possible wife. Then here you are, pregnant with my child, willing to share your life with someone called Charlie of all things to give that child a father—so why would you not marry me?'

Mel tried desperately to think of a valid response but he touched his finger to her lips before she could frame a single word.

'You wish to keep working—you can do that here. We are setting up the paediatric surgical unit—it will be yours to order and staff as you wish. And while you work you can rest easy about the child. Children are brought up, to a large extent, in the women's house—going between there and their parents' houses as happily as the young kids play among a goat herd. You will have your child yet when you are working you will know he or she is in a secure and happy family environment—in an environment of love.'

Here was something she could refute.

'You weren't,' she reminded him. 'You were sent overseas to school at six.'

'Which is why,' he said, his voice cold, 'my child will not suffer in that way. Oh, I have doubts, too, Melissa. What kind of father will I, who never knew a father's love, make? I have real doubts, but that will not stop me doing the best I can.'

'Oh, Arun,' she said softly, and reached up to wrap her arms around his shoulders.

She sounded so genuinely unhappy for him Arun sat up, turned on a bedside light and looked at her properly. She was beautiful—flushed and rosy, her wild hair splayed across the pillow, her pale body with its nest of curls beneath the barely swollen belly the source of such delight…

But this reluctance to give in to marriage…

'You like me?'

It seemed a strange question to be asking after they'd made love so satisfactorily, but it seemed important to find out.

She nodded, opened her reddened lips to add words then closed them again, allowing him to continue.

'We're good together in bed?'

Another nod, this time with a slight smile that made him want to take her again—right now.

But he couldn't do that—not until a lot of things were sorted out.

'So why are you hesitant about marriage?'

Mel looked at him. Long and lean, but well muscled with the leanness because he could lift and hold her with ease, although she was no lightweight. Intelligent, caring—his love-making showed that—apparently wealthy, if what she'd seen at the party was any indication, great in bed, so why not marry him?

Because he didn't love her! How could he when he was still in love with the memory of his beautiful young wife? It would be like competing with a ghost...

The answer came so unexpectedly and was so pathetic Mel decided it must be wrong. She was thirty-five. Surely she wasn't still lost in a dream of finding the perfect love?

But it was the only answer she could find to explain why she was so hesitant.

'I can't explain,' she said, then she added, 'And now I have to sleep. I have to see Tia's baby in the morning, then it's Jenny's wedding in the afternoon. Are you staying or going?'

'Staying or going?' he repeated.

'In my bed.'

And as she said the words she wondered again why they'd ended up in her bedroom, not his, but this time the obvious answer came to her—his bed was the one he'd shared with his wife, the wife he'd loved.

With a sigh that hid the sudden surge of sadness in her heart, she turned over on her side, pulled the sheet up to her shoulder, tucked her hands beneath her head and prepared to go to sleep.

She felt the bed move and thought he was leaving

but then his body curved around hers, warming her back, and his hand rested gently on her hip.

'Technically, this *is* my bed,' he whispered, nestling closer, reminding her of how good it had been, four months ago, to have him sleep beside her.

He should have gone back to his own room. He knew that. But he also knew he wanted, more than was wise, to sleep with her again. Just sleep. At least until the morning, when anything might happen, and probably would...

CHAPTER SEVEN

MAKING love in the morning, Mel decided as she stood in the large shower with Arun making soapy circles on her back, was probably one of the nicest things in the whole wide world. She had set aside her worries about the future and what it might hold, refusing to think about Arun's suggestions until she was on her own and could think clearly. So right now she was relaxed and at ease and ready to take on whatever the world had to offer her right here and now, although if he kept soaping there, taking on stuff might be a bit delayed.

'I have to get to work,' she scolded him, and he laughed, then turned her so she faced him.

'You do not have to go to work!' he told her sternly, although the words lost a little of their firmness with the hot water streaming all around them.

'But I do—there are things to organise if we're operating here, and the baby to see. I do wish he had a name— Oh!'

The thought was so shocking she forgot about playing with Arun in the shower and stepped out, winding one towel around her hair and drying herself on another.

'Do you think,' she asked, as Arun turned off the water and stepped out himself, 'that she doesn't want to give him the name they chose because she's still uncertain that he'll live? How awful if she's thinking that way. How unhappy she must be!'

Arun shook his head.

'Despite a plenitude of sisters, I have not and will not ever understand women. How could you be thinking of Tia's happiness or otherwise while we were in the shower?'

Mel smiled at his disbelief.

'Multi-tasking?' she responded, tucking one towel around her body then taking the one off her hair to rub at the wet tangled mess. 'It's a woman thing! See, I can dry my hair, wonder how long it will take to get the tangles out, plan out the day—I'll see Tia's baby first but later I'm going to need to work out exactly how we'll do the operation. And when do you work? See patients? You seemed to be looking after me most of yesterday.'

He stared at her for a little longer, then shook his head, wrapped a towel around his waist and left the bathroom, poking his head back in long enough to say, 'I'll tell Olara breakfast in ten minutes—does that suit your schedule?'

Mel's towel had slipped so she wadded it and threw it at him, then saw the desire leap again in his eyes and knew it was a mistake. But easing that desire would have to wait—there was so much to be done.

A young man was in the ICU room with the baby—a doctor from A and E, Arun explained, relieving Sarah until another paediatric registrar could be brought on staff. Arun took Tia to one side as Mel examined her small patient, smiling as she realised the little one was doing well.

'How can you tell? What do you look for?' Tia asked, and before Mel could explain, Arun took the chart and carefully pointed out to his sister the different measurements and what they meant, assuring her the baby was more than holding his own.

'See,' he said, gently, 'he has even gained some weight.'

Tia hugged him hard, then hugged Mel as well, before changing the subject to ask about the party. Had Mel enjoyed it? Had Jenny looked beautiful?

'It was great and Jenny looked gorgeous,' Mel assured her, happy that Tia was showing an interest in things other than the baby. They talked for a while, Zaffra, the nurse, returning to take over as the baby-watcher.

The young doctor from A and E remained near the door, hovering with some purpose, Mel suspected. Then Arun spoke to him and frowned at the young man's reply.

'What is it?' Mel asked.

'He was wondering if you could spare some time to go down to the A and E department,' Arun replied, although he still looked perplexed.

'If he and the other doctors sharing duty with Sarah are from there, they might want to know more about the baby's condition,' Mel suggested. 'I'm only too happy to go down, but someone will have to point the way. I've a feeling I could get lost in this place for ever if left on my own.'

'I shall be your guide,' Arun said, investing the words with a deeper meaning so Mel found herself not only shivering but thinking thoughts that should be far from her head in a hospital situation.

'Don't you have a job to go to?' she teased, hoping to hide her reaction.

'It will wait for me,' he said easily, then added, 'Though not for much longer. Come, the baby is being well cared for. We will go.'

Mel followed him, trying to take note of the corridors along which they passed, feeling she no longer knew which way was up and which down.

Feeling she no longer knew where she was in

other ways as well. Was Arun serious about marriage?

She watched him as he paused to exchange words with a colleague.

Would it work?

As he'd said, marriages of convenience had worked in his country for centuries so he saw no reason for it not to work.

Yet he'd married Hussa for love…

'Now, this one takes us down,' he said, ushering her inside, and nodding to those already packed in the lift.

A polite man, but used to command.

If they did marry, then her biggest—and most irrational, she had to admit—fear would be allayed. Should something happen to her, her child would have Jenny to be a mother to him or her, and that was a far better option than leaving Charlie holding the baby…

It would, in fact, be the perfect solution.

'And down this corridor.'

He pushed open the double doors into the A and E department. And for a moment Mel could only stare, for the room in front of her was jam-packed with people, women, she now saw, women and children. Some babies in arms, some older children, but everywhere black-clad women, most of them with their faces masked or veiled, holding children.

A young man in a short white coat, stetho-scope dangling from his pocket, rushed towards them, speaking not to her but to Arun.

'We didn't tell them,' he said helplessly. 'Somehow word just got around that there was a baby doctor in the city. They've come from everywhere, even desert people. There are *camels* parked outside.'

'Camels?' she said, the thought making her turn and smile at Arun, but he was staring at the crowd and shaking his head, a look of profound sadness on his face.

'What is it, Arun?' she demanded as the young man moved away to speak to a woman who was bringing her baby forward.

'It is shame, Melissa, that I did not know—we did not know, Kam and I—how very bad things are here. We thought we had time to fix the wrongs, but look at this. I must get help here quickly, must get onto the other paediatricians we have contracted to start shortly. The list is back in my office. Come, it is not your problem.'

'Not my problem? Women with sick children are not my problem? Of course they are. Now, where's that young man gone? He needs to get them organised. Do the nurses understand triage? I'll be more use to children with heart problems, so maybe if I see them first while the other doctors on duty do the initial examination of the others and pass on anything serious to me. Can we get Sarah Craig down here? As long as I'm in the hospital, she doesn't need to be with Tia's baby.'

Arun stared at her in disbelief.

'You *can't* do this!' he said.

She shook her head and smiled.

'That's where you're wrong. This is one thing I *can* do, and if I'm staying here for two weeks to operate on Tia's baby, I can work here for the next two weeks, maybe four because I can't leave straight after the op. That should give you and

Kam time to set up your paeds ward and get it staffed, OK? Now, find me the young man, and a nurse who can translate for me, and let me get to work.'

It was Arun's turn to shake his head, but Mel knew there wasn't a moment to be wasted if she wanted to see even half of these women today and still get to Jenny's wedding.

'Shoo!' she said, and made a pushing motion with her hands.

He stared at her, his chin tilting upward as if to defy her order. Who, after all, was *she* to be giving orders to a sheikh? Then he smiled.

'I'm shooing,' he said quietly, but his eyes said something else. His eyes said, Thank you, though the gratitude was still tinged with shame.

And seeing that expression, knowing the beating his pride must be taking as he realised the extent to which his people had been ne-glected, her heart ached for him…

By lunchtime she had seven children lined up for radiological examinations but because the radiology staff had been hired for their skills with adults, not children, she wanted to be in the room with the children being scanned.

'I need to see for myself,' she explained to Arun, who had appeared from nowhere to insist she stop working to eat lunch. 'And I won't get them all done this afternoon because we have to get to the wedding. As well as that, some of the little ones might need to be sedated, so maybe in the morning, if I could have time in the radiology rooms and whatever staff are available, we can work through the day.'

He sighed and shook his head.

'I don't want you doing this,' he said, and she smiled at him.

'Liar! What you mean is that you feel bad that it is me doing it when I came over for a week of fun and celebration of Jenny's wedding. But, in fact, you're delighted to have someone who *can* do this.'

'And mortified to see the extent of the need,' he said quietly, the pain in his words so clear she could feel it. 'My father was ill for a long time before he died, but he kept control of what he could. He allowed the foreigners to spend their money where and how they wanted but he actively discouraged the local people from using any of these facilities. The wealthy families, of course, weren't swayed by this, and instead of going to Europe for their medical and dental treatment, they welcomed the new hospital and its attendant services, but we have always been a people who have shared whatever we've had, so this division between those who have the best and those who have nothing is very much against our traditional ways.'

Mel thought of the compound with huge houses encircling the inner courtyard and wondered about traditional ways, and Arun, perhaps guessing her thoughts, continued.

'People see our family—the houses we have— as wealthy, but our compound is like a city, housing maybe three hundred people, many families, all living together. And if some work at one thing, preparing food and serving it, others, like Miriam, work at other things. She has made the loose trousers the children wear for as long as I can remember. Even my mother, who thought herself a princess and above work, made perfumes for everyone in the family, including those you might see as servants. It is our way.'

It is our way! Such simple words, but like the pain she'd heard earlier it pierced Mel's heart and for an instant she felt regret that he didn't love her, for it would be so very easy for her to love him…

Especially if they were married…

Satisfied that she had eaten well, Arun escorted Melissa first to the ICU where the baby continued to do well then back to A and E where still more women waited with their children.

'It's impossible!' he said. 'You'll never see them all. We'll have to leave by four to drive out for the wedding and you need to wash and dress. You should stop now.'

She checked her watch then smiled at him.

'Give me until three. I'll leave then. And this is worse than it looks. I've seen a lot of these children, their mothers are just waiting for follow-up appointments or medication. The staff here have been overwhelmed but they're doing a great job handling so many people at once— and the children, they are so good, waiting patiently with their mothers.'

'We are good at patience,' Arun told her, and knew by the flush that rose in her cheeks that she'd understood the double meaning in his words.

Would she marry him?

She hadn't said no, which gave him hope, but she certainly hadn't leapt at the idea.

And she was speaking in terms of staying four weeks, which wasn't a good sign.

Although surely a woman as intelligent as she was would see all the positives of such a union?

So why hadn't she said yes?

Was she fonder of this paragon Charlie than she admitted?

Anger fired and he knew he had to find a solution for it was unthinkable that another man should rear his child.

He set the subject aside, although he realised it must have been preying on his subconscious mind when, later, they settled into the car to take them back to the compound for the wedding.

Melissa was wearing a long gown in the palest blue, with darker blue flowers embroidered wildly all over it. A darker blue shawl hid her vibrant hair, making her eyes look bluer and her skin creamier. He wanted to tell her how beautiful she was, but saying it then asking her again about the marriage option might make the compliment sound hollow.

'Jenny's wedding,' he began, wondering how to approach the subject again, and surprised at his own unfamiliar hesitation. 'Has it made you think of my suggestion?'

Blue eyes studied him, and the smile he so enjoyed flitted momentarily across her lips.

'No,' she said, and smiled properly now. 'That's answering your question literally—Jenny's wedding has made no difference to my thinking but yes to what you're really asking. I have been giving your proposition some thought.'

Proposition?

'It was a proposal,' he said stiffly, angered that

she seemed to be making a joke of a situation he found so difficult.

The smile disappeared.

'I would have thought a proposal had an element of love in it, Arun,' she said quietly, and once again he was struck by how little he understood the female half of the human race.

Which made him even more irritated.

'You were willing to accept Charlie without love—without even attraction, from what you tell me,' he snapped, then regretted opening his mouth for he'd sounded petty even to his own ears.

Once again she studied him, although now there was no hint of a smile.

'That was intended to be a safeguard for the baby. I have no family and Jenny, my best friend, at the time I decided on it, was committed to travelling to far-off places. I needed to know there was someone to take care of the baby if anything happened to me.'

'And you chose this Charlie, not the baby's father!'

Had she heard the anger simmering close to rage that she put her hand on his and said his name? All she said was 'Arun!' but it was enough to calm him slightly.

'I didn't know you'd be interested,' she added quietly. 'When we met you'd been adamant children weren't in your future. I had to make some contingency plans—just in case.'

He heard a quaver in her voice as she spoke and the uncertainty of it killed the remnants of his anger. Now it was his turn to study her, to remember something she'd said earlier—something about fear, about terror.

'Why don't you have a family?' he asked, but knew the question had come too late. The car had stopped and the crowds gathered in the compound were looking expectantly towards it.

Today there even more people around, all obviously in their best attire, although a lot of the women wore black gowns over their colourful dresses, the purples, blues and richest greens peeping shyly at the hemlines or the sleeves.

'This is the extended family, all of our people,

come to celebrate with Kam and Jenny,' Arun explained, taking Mel's hand to lead her up the steps.

But when he was waylaid, someone touching his sleeve to attract his attention then talking to him urgently, she went on ahead, knowing there'd be someone somewhere to show her where she had to go.

Miriam rescued her, taking her arm and leading her to where Jenny was being prepared by a multitude of sisters.

'Look,' Jen said, holding up her hands to show a hennaed pattern on them.

'That's beautiful,' Mel told her, seeing the delicacy of the tracing of leaves and buds.

'We'd do it to you but it's too late,' Jen told her. 'You have to mix it to a paste and put it on thickly then hold it near heat to dry it so it leaves the stain on the skin. See Miriam's feet.'

Miriam lifted one foot to show the hennaed sole.

'I didn't do my feet because they're too ticklish to have someone painting them,' Jen explained.

Mel saw the happiness in her friend's face and heard the delight in her voice and was so glad for her. That Jen, who'd suffered so much with the loss of her husband and unborn son, should find such joy again was a miracle, but while Mel was happy for her, she also felt a tiny twinge of not jealousy but regret that this joy had found Jen twice while somehow it had bypassed her completely.

She closed her eyes against the thought and found an image of Arun on the inside of her eyelids. Just his face, strong and clean-cut, the dark brows above his green eyes, the beautiful lips, moving, telling her they'd marry.

She blinked him away, although she knew in reality it would take more than a blink to get rid of him.

Especially now…

Then Jen was ready, her beautiful blue silk gown covered with a black one, her unbound golden hair covered with a black veil so she looked like a black parcel, wrapped ready for her husband to unwrap. The women escorted her out of the room into the big room where Jane and Bob Stapleton came forward to greet her with a kiss. Then everyone was shuffled into place, Mel beside Arun one step behind the bride and groom, and the ceremony began.

Had Kam explained what would be said to Jen before this started? Mel wondered, listening to the music of the words and understanding none of them, but what she did understand was a gasp from the crowd of people in the room, and she turned to Arun, eyebrows raised, hoping there was enough of a murmur going on behind them for him to explain.

Which he promptly did!

'He is saying there might be another wedding in the family soon,' he said, his eyes daring her to argue, to make a scene in front of what must have been several hundred people.

'Yours?' Her whisper might have been quiet but it was definitely a demand.

'Of course,' he said.

Mel looked around desperately. On one side white-gowned men stood, most with prayer beads clicking through their fingers. On the other side the women, like bright butterflies, their black veils dispensed with because all the men present counted as family.

There was no help at hand but she wasn't going to give in just like that.

'I'm not marrying you!' she muttered at Arun, who turned with a smile and murmured,

'He didn't say who I was to marry.'

'Oh!'

She felt flat—deflated—although she'd known he had to marry. He'd promised Jen…

Then his smile broadened and somehow sneaked beneath Mel's guard, warming and exciting her at the same time.

'But I haven't given up on my first choice,' he told her. 'Have you not heard the legends? The stories of the desert sheikh who takes the woman of his desires and rides off with his bride across his saddle? Shall we ride in the morning?'

The question was as seductive as his touch had been the previous night, and Mel found her body trembling with remembered desire.

How could he do this to her, with no more than words and glances? And how could they be having this conversation in the middle of Jen's wedding? All around them people were chanting now, rhythmic words Mel didn't understand, while Arun alternately joined in and spoke to her, tormenting her with his special magic, moving close enough for their bodies to be touching.

And how could she fight him when he had such an effect on all her senses?

No, not all her senses—surely she retained some common sense!

'I'm not the woman of your desires,' Mel said, edging away from him to evade his touch. 'And as for riding off across the desert, this is the twenty-first century in case you didn't know.'

'Oh, I know it,' he said, still smiling and still exciting her traitorous body. 'And I applaud what the new age has brought with it, but men and women still meet and are attracted. Can you deny that?'

'Attraction's not enough as the basis for a marriage,' Mel muttered at him.

'But attraction, combined with a baby on the way, surely is.'

Was that true?

Or was it a false presumption that would lead to certain disaster?

Mel looked around at the people gathered in the room, at the children, some standing quietly, others playing, also quietly, all of them happy and healthy, secure in this, to Mel, strange environment.

'Secure'—that was the killer word. What Arun was offering was security for her baby, security that went far beyond anything else Mel could put in place—security that eased the terror hidden in her heart.

She slid a glance towards Arun, ignored the shivers of desire, and studied his face.

Given his own childhood, she knew beyond a doubt he would provide the best possible life for this child, and his best would be a wondrous thing. But he would also give it the love that had been missing from his own life.

He might not be able to give Mel love, but the child, she knew without a doubt, would always know his or her father's love. That love tipped the scales.

She sighed.

'Yes, I'll ride with you in the morning,' she said, thinking to tell him then, where she'd first told him of the baby.

He seemed startled and she realised it had been a long time since he'd asked the question, but then he smiled and she knew he'd guessed her thoughts.

People began moving, Jenny was whisked away. Mel wondered whether she should follow, but Arun gripped her arm.

'Jenny will be dressed in the golden headdress and collar of the family now. It is very heavy but it is the bride's gift, so to speak, her financial future should things not work out between her and Kam. She has to wear it for a short time so everyone can marvel at it, then she and Kam will leave. Normally, they would go to the bride room and stay there for a week.'

The look that accompanied these last words made Mel's skin heat, but she hid her reaction as she was fascinated by this glimpse of a different culture.

'And then,' she asked, 'does she live with Kam or in the women's house?'

Arun smiled.

'Can you imagine your friend wanting to live separate to her husband? If you can, I assure you I can't imagine Kam wanting to spend any un-avoidable time apart from Jenny. In the past, when men like my father had up to four wives, all the wives lived in the women's house, having specific nights they spent with their husband. Their husband was supposed to treat all of them equally, but that didn't always happen. Miriam was my father's favourite and she could have played up to that, but she is a fine woman and made sure the other wives were happy, or at least contented with their lot. But as well as wives, there are aunts and grandmothers and women who may not be related but are friends from long ago. Many women live there—it is the hub of the compound. Everything is organised from there, as far as family is concerned, and that way the men are free for business dealings.'

'It's very different,' Mel said, but she could

understand how the tradition would have grown, the women crowded together for safety while their menfolk were away.

Then Jenny returned with such a weight of gold jewellery on her head and around her neck that she needed Kam's support to walk.

'Take a good look at it,' she said to Mel, 'because I'll give it ten minutes at the most then it's coming off. It's a wonder all the married women don't have tendonitis.'

Jenny paraded around the room, men and women nodding their approval, then she and Kam disappeared, to spend their first night as man and wife in a hotel in the city, and the partying began.

Mel was on a settee by the wall, listening to the Stapletons' latest account of their exploration of Zaheer, when Arun approached.

He excused himself to the Stapletons, put out his hand and drew Mel to her feet, his eyes studying her face.

'You are ready to leave?' he said, surprising her, for although she was feeling exhausted after a night of love-making and a hard day's work, she had doubted he would leave the party until it was finished.

'I am,' she admitted, 'but there's no need for you to leave as well. I'd like to go back to the hospital to check the baby before I go to bed, but all I need is a car and driver.'

'And another in the morning to bring you back so you can ride?' He smiled, not his seductive smile but the kind one that made her feel weak and woozy inside. 'I have just returned from the hospital. The baby is doing well. Your clothes are still in Jenny's house. You can spend the night there.'

Alone? she wondered, and was surprised by the spurt of disappointment she felt. But, of course, it would be alone. Arun would be unlikely to cause a scandal in this obviously close-knit community by spending the night with her.

So Mel did the only thing she could, she thanked him and allowed him to lead her out of the big building and across the courtyard towards Jenny and Kam's house.

'I can't believe it's only three days since I arrived and we walked through here,' she said, looking up to where the full moon rode high in the sky, visible in spite of the lights in the compound.

'Three days since I kissed you just here,' Arun whispered, drawing her into the side passage where they'd talked—and kissed.

But not like this. Not with heat and passion and an intensity that burned through Mel, made hotter and brighter and harder because tonight they wouldn't take their kisses to the logical conclusion…

CHAPTER EIGHT

MEL woke to the sound of Keira's gentle voice urging her to wake up. The spacious room was still dark, although the young woman had turned on the bathroom light so Mel could see the doorway and pick out various pieces of furniture as she slowly remembered where she was and why.

'You are riding?' Keira asked, and Mel nodded, then realised a tray, set with a teapot and cup and a plate of pastries, had been place on the bedside table. 'You might like something to eat before you go.'

Mel thanked her and poured a cup of tea, although now she was fully awake she remembered why she'd agreed to ride with Arun, and a feeling somewhere between excitement and apprehension churned in her stomach.

Setting down the tea, barely tasted, she left the bed and hurried into the bathroom, wanting to shower and get out to the stables—wanting to tell him before she lost her nerve!

He was waiting where he'd been last time, although this time there were two horses saddled.

'Haven't lost your nerve?' he said, echoing her thoughts so perfectly she could only stare at him.

How had he known she intended telling him this morning?

Or that her answer would be yes?

Although maybe she'd have been just as nervous over saying no.

'I have no idea what you're talking about,' she said, refusing to acknowledge his cleverness.

He smiled and held Mershinga while Mel mounted.

Would she read his doubt behind his smile? Arun wondered, thinking of the preparations he had made and wondering if they were all for naught.

But as he mounted Saracen he glanced towards the woman he hoped to soon make his wife and knew he hadn't guessed wrong, although she certainly didn't seem overwhelmingly happy about her decision to marry him.

In fact, she seemed very tense, her face pale, her lips set—more like someone going to the gallows than a woman contemplating marriage.

Which bothered him, although, thinking about it, if she was willing to go to this Charlie for security, surely what he, Arun, was offering, was more appealing.

They rode out of the compound and he heard her sigh and saw her stiffly held shoulders relax as she eased Mershinga to a halt and looked around.

And now he did know what she was thinking, for the look of wonder on her face told him as clearly as writing on a pad. He sat beside her, filled with joy that she could see and appreciate the beauty of the desert.

'You said rosy-tipped and I didn't take it in,' she breathed, whispering the words as if afraid noise might break the spell of early morning.

'But, look, the dunes are rosy, dark beneath and rosy-tipped, just as you said, the colour changing to gold while we watch.'

She eased her mount forward so the horse picked its way slowly across the sand, Arun falling in behind, content to watch her wide-eyed wonder at the spectacle.

They rode to the cairn where she'd told him of the baby, and there, as she was about to dismount, he joined her, stopping further movement with a hand on her arm.

'You have come here to answer me?' he asked.

She turned and looked at him, looking up as Mershinga was a full three hands shorter than his black stallion.

'I have,' Mel answered solemnly.

'You'll marry me,' Arun asked, a tightening in his gut suggesting he was really anxious about this.

'I will,' Mel said, and although he watched her as she spoke he could read no sign of joy in the declaration.

But joy would come in time, he decided, for

this was a good thing in so many ways. Enough for now she had agreed and they could celebrate.

'Then come,' he said. 'We won't stop here this morning. We'll ride a little further.'

He led the way, guiding Saracen up the steep sandstone slope behind the wadi, knowing Mershinga would follow. At the top the land levelled out and it was here he'd asked his people to set out the picnic. He pulled Saracen to one side of the track and waited until Mel reached the top, then enjoyed again the look of wonder in her eyes for from here she could see the desert spread in front of her, wave upon wave of dunes and cliffs, while behind her the city was bathed in the golden rays of the rising sun, the new buildings sparkling like jewels in the morning light.

'A tent?' Mel said, looking behind her now at the strange black shape.

'A picnic just for us, to celebrate our engagement,' Arun said, and the doubt that had been nagging at Mel ever since she'd made up her mind the previous night now returned—full strength.

'It's not really an engagement,' she protested. 'We're doing this for the baby—a marriage of convenience—you said so yourself.'

Arun had dismounted, tied the stallion's reins to a hitching post by the tent, and was now holding Mershinga's head, waiting for Mel to join him at ground level.

'Then we shall celebrate you agreeing to marry me,' he said, apparently unperturbed by her downgrading of their arrangement.

She slid off the horse, glancing uneasily towards the small tent, not sure whether to be disappointed or relieved when a white-clad attendant appeared in the doorway, unrolling a brightly coloured rug onto the sand in front of it.

'Come,' Arun said, taking her arm and leading her forward. 'For you today the best Zaheer can offer—breakfast in the dunes.'

He was so obviously proud of his country Mel weakened, turning to him with a teasing smile.

'The best? Better than the desert by moonlight?'

'It too is the best,' he said, so seriously she felt a little hitch in her heart and knew again how very easy it would be to love him…

They sat cross-legged on the carpet while the attendant prepared the special savoury pancakes Mel had eaten at the apartment. But these, cooked over a small brazier, were even more delicious, the yoghurt served with them thicker and creamier, the spice tastes more tantalising.

Or was it the company that made it all seem special?

She glanced sideways at Arun and caught him watching her.

'Your family,' he said quietly. 'You didn't answer me yesterday. An accident? Divorce?'

Mel shook her head.

'You will tell me?'

He phrased it as a question but she heard it as…not a demand so much as a need to know, and realised he deserved the truth.

'My mother died when I was born, my father opted not to have anything to do with a newborn baby who had, in his eyes, killed his wife. His family also turned away—supporting him, I think, rather than outright rejecting me. My mother's mother took me and raised me, and she died two years ago.'

Mel shrugged to show it no longer mattered and most of the time it didn't, but when Arun put his arm around her and drew her close she felt the loss again and had to swallow hard.

'You told me you were terrified, and I didn't understand. Yet you went ahead with this pregnancy?' he said, and she realised it wasn't her lack of family that had drawn his sympathy but his understanding of her stupid fears.

'It's such a rare occurrence these days it's hardly likely to happen twice in two generations,' she said, then added the bald truth. 'And it wasn't so much fear of dying that freaked me out, but leaving behind a child with no one to care for it.'

'Hence Charlie,' Arun murmured, more to himself than Melissa, as understanding of her situation not only dawned on him but caused him actual pain.

He moved slightly away on the pretext of passing her a plate of fruit.

So she *had* said yes to his proposal as the best option for her child.

And what was wrong with that?

Hadn't he couched his proposal as an offer of security for both her and the child?

Wasn't this what he wanted? A marriage of convenience?

He knew it was, knew the attraction was an added bonus, so why was he feeling perturbed?

Because it put him on the same level as this Charlie she spoke of—a bloodless wimp who would settle for marriage without the love of this strong, resourceful, beautiful and sexy woman.

She was talking of the children she wished to see again in A and E, of radiology appointments, but he couldn't get his mind around her conversation while his heart—no, it couldn't possibly be his heart, it had to be his pride—was suffering.

'I will arrange it,' he promised, although the promise he made to himself was very different.

He would change her thinking. He would woo

and win her so she came to him in marriage wanting *him*, not a job or a safe haven for her child.

And that reminded him of her fear and he put his arm around her again, and held her as the sun's rays warmed the sands and the dawn slipped quietly into day.

'We should go,' Mel said, though having acceded to the marriage idea and with her hunger satisfied she felt pleasantly relaxed and could have sat on the carpet with Arun's arms around her for a very long time. 'I've got work to do and I'm sure you have as well.'

She edged away, standing up and shaking sand from her loose trousers, then, remembering it was less than twenty-four hours since Jenny's wedding, she turned to him.

'I don't want a big-deal wedding with all those people,' she said. 'You must have easier ways to get married here. A place where just the two of us can go?'

He smiled the lazy smile that started a quiver in her chest and said, 'You'll deny our people an excuse to party?'

'They've been partying all week for Jenny's wedding,' Mel reminded him. 'That's more than enough.'

Then something, maybe the quiver she'd felt earlier, prompted her to add, 'Our wedding's different anyway. It's a convenience, remember.'

Arun's face was raised to look at her, and the morning sun was shining on it, so she saw the shadow that passed across it, although usually his emotions were as carefully masked as the faces of the veiled women.

Did he not like being reminded that that's what it was?

Would he rather pretend it was a love match?

No, he was far too practical to think that way. Wasn't he?

Mel pondered the question as they rode back to the compound where she showered hurriedly and dressed—again in loose trousers and tunic top, though thinking that she'd have to tell Jenny about the pregnancy and marriage fairly soon.

Before everyone knew…

The car was waiting at the door, Arun standing beside it.

Mel tried to read his expression but once again his face was wiped of all emotion.

Did the women wear masks and veils because they had less success at hiding their feelings than the men, although surely their eyes, the so-called windows of the soul, would give their emotions away?

'You are worried about the children?' Arun asked, as the driver steered the car through the compound gates.

Mel turned to him.

'Was I frowning?' she asked, and before he could reply she explained, 'I was thinking of masks and veils and whether as well as hiding beauty they hide emotion.'

Arun studied her for a moment, then smiled.

'Or perhaps conceal it so only the most persistent of lovers can penetrate the screen.'

Mel nodded slowly.

'So love is the key?' she said, her voice so quiet he barely heard the words.

And when he did make sense of them—literal sense—he wasn't sure he understood what she was saying.

Neither was he about to find out because she was speaking again, more loudly this time.

'How do I move around the hospital? Even when I know my way somewhere, like to the apartment or to A and E, how do I get access?'

Could she switch from talk of love to talk of work so swiftly?

Because that's all it was? Talk?

He didn't like the idea, but he, too, could make the switch.

'I will get you a key card that has your ID on it—it will get you wherever you want to go in the hospital and will also open the door to the apartment,' he said, then he muttered away in his own language for a moment, explaining as they arrived at the hospital that he must be as stupid as she was, so calmly accepting that she would continue working here.

'It is not your job,' he added, though he knew it was futile.

Out of the car now, she turned and smiled at him.
'Ah, but it will be—that's the whole point.'

'If you mean of our marriage, I am not marrying you to get a good paediatrician on staff. Kam and I had already interviewed someone who will make an excellent head of paediatrics. If you wish to work, then having you set up a paediatric surgical unit would be a bonus for our people.'

He knew he was speaking stiffly—hopefully not pompously—but her attitude to their marriage was grating on him. Not that he'd expected honeyed tones and melting glances, but they shared a strong attraction so surely a sense of—fondness? warmth?—wouldn't hurt!

Mel raised her eyebrows at him, aware he wasn't happy but unsure why. Did he want her to pretend it was a love match?

She shook her head in denial of her thoughts, knowing, the way she was beginning to think about him, that such a pretence would be dangerous for it would be too close to the real thing.

Thinking in terms of the convenience was much better, and remembering it was for security for her baby, not for the joy of being in Arun's company, was far, far safer for her mental well-being.

She followed him towards the main foyer, putting thoughts of love and marriage out of her mind—screening them off—determined this time to notice where they were going so she could begin to find her own way around the hospital.

'Do you want to go up to the apartment?'

Expressionless face, voice devoid of emotion, yet still Mel shivered, thinking of what could happen should they go up to the apartment—remembering how good it would feel to be in his arms again.

'Best not,' she said, hoping her own face was as expressionless as his. 'Maybe the ICU then A and E. I've got a lot of those children I saw yesterday lined up for tests and scans, so I'll need to see them again, then there are all the others.'

They were walking towards the lift and she noticed the corridor that led to A and E.

'You spoke of clinics in different areas and I'm sure you mentioned hospitals, plural, when

we spoke earlier, so why have these children not
been seen somewhere else?'

She stood beside him while Arun pressed the
button for the lift, a frown lowering his dark
eyebrows.

'I wondered that myself, so I asked, and found
they do not trust the other hospital—the old one
which Kam and I have been trying to remodel bit
by bit—because they say their children get
sicker there than they are before they go in. And
at the new one, this one, there have been no
women doctors in the A and E department—I did
not realise that—and a lot of the women who
came yesterday are tribal women, not city
women, and they did not want to talk with a man
who wasn't a relative. There are baby clinics in
the country, and here in the city, where women
take their babies and a nurse will treat the child
or give advice, but when the advice was to take
the child to see a doctor, they held back.'

'Poor things,' Mel said, and Arun must have
heard genuine empathy in her voice for he turned
towards her.

'Poor things?'

He looked so worried she put a hand on his sleeve.

'To believe there is something wrong with your child and not be able to talk to someone about it.'

Arun nodded, but once again guilt was gnawing at him. That he hadn't known things were so bad—that he'd travelled the world to learn more in his specialty while at home facilities were so poor women were unable to get help for their sick children.

But it was useless feeling anger at the old man who, even ill, had clung to his power, refusing to allow his sons to fully modernise the old hospital or to nationalise the new hospital so free services could be provided to everyone.

'We will fix things,' he said, making the words a promise, knowing he would keep it.

They made their way to the ICU room where the baby was. Mel stopped at the door and stared around in disbelief. The pristine white room had been transformed into a fairyland, with toys, mobiles, posters and cards making it so vibrantly alive Mel had to blink a couple of times before she could take it all in.

'I can't believe it,' she said, turning to Arun who had obviously seen the decorations the previous evening when he'd come in.

'Just because the family cannot be here with Tia and the baby, it doesn't mean they can't send gifts.'

'Well, they've certainly done that,' Mel agreed, making her way to the crib where Sarah Craig was waiting to hand over the baby's chart.

The baby was doing far better than Mel had hoped, and she told Tia, adding, 'I'm sure it's all the attention you are giving him that is making him stronger every day.'

Tia beamed at her.

'My mother's attention too and soon his father's for my husband is coming back to be with me when the baby has the operation—is that not wonderful news?'

'The very best,' Mel agreed, giving Tia a hug.

Then she turned to Sarah.

'If you can get someone, a nurse would do, to relieve you, I could use your help again down-stairs in A and E.'

'All but done,' Sarah told her. 'I've only been waiting for you to arrive. There's a nurse standing by to take over here. She's done a shift with the baby before so she knows what to watch for.' She glanced at Arun. 'If that's OK with Dr al'Kawali,' she added, smiling at him.

Mel wasn't sure if Sarah was checking with her nominal boss that this arrangement had his approval or pandering to him because he was such a handsome and sexy man.

And surely the squirmy feeling in Mel's stomach couldn't be jealousy...

Had she seen five hundred babies and small children? It certainly felt that way. As he had the previous day, at some stage Arun had appeared and drawn her off to a small sitting room, ordering her to sit, to eat, to drink some fruit juice or tea.

Sarah had worked in tandem with her through

the morning, but had disappeared before Mel went to lunch, presumably to return to the ICU.

Or maybe she'd been off duty, working to a roster because she was actually employed by the hospital.

Though Mel doubted that would be the case. Most doctors she knew would keep working while there were still patients to be seen.

'Who's next?' Mel asked the young nurse who'd been helping her all day.

'No more,' the woman said. 'His Excellency says no more.'

'His Excellency?'

'The sheikh—Dr Rahman al'Kawali—he says no more. They must come back tomorrow or the next day. The women at the reception counter are even now making times for them to come. His Excellency says you must stop before you are exhausted.'

Dark eyes looked anxiously into Mel's.

'You will do this—stop—or he will be very angry.'

'Oh, will he, now?' Mel said, then realised she couldn't bring Arun's wrath down on this poor defenceless woman's head. 'And have you seen him very angry?'

The woman shook her head.

'But I have heard. It does not happen often, but when things are not as they should be—the floor soiled, or the staff careless—then he can be angry. Justly so, of course.'

Of course, Mel echoed silently, remembering how angry he had been when she'd told him about Charlie—coldly angry.

She closed her eyes for a moment, trying to blot out the memory, and opened them to find not the nurse but Arun—the sometimes angry sheikh—standing in front of her.

'So, you are ready to go?'

'Back up to the apartment? Do you mind me staying there? It seems easiest, but if it's a nuisance or is breaking some rule for engaged couples or might offend someone—I'm sorry, I'm a bit muddled at the moment.'

He made an exasperated noise and seized her hand, dragging her out of A and E, back into the small room where she'd eaten lunch.

'You can't keep working like this,' he stormed. 'It's not right—and it's too much for you.'

Disconcerted by the grasp he still had on her hand, Mel tried to ease away.

'If you add "in your condition", I'll scream.'

To her surprise he smiled, and as the stern, rather forbidding face softened with the smile, all the reasons she shouldn't be so close—shouldn't be touching him—stirred to life again, firing every nerve in her body, so when he drew her closer, she didn't resist. In fact, far from it. She let her body slump against his, feeding on his strength.

'And will this draw such a fierce reaction?' he asked softly, his eyes holding hers as his lips moved closer, claiming her mouth with a hunger that burned like fever through her body.

'Arun, no...'

The protest died on her lips, for his hands were now smoothing across the loose fabric of her shirt, and her sensitive breasts were responding to the teasing touch, her nipples hardening to buds that sought more than teasing.

'The apartment...' she managed to murmur, and

he eased away, taking her elbow and guiding her out of the room. Mel was in such a daze, or haze perhaps, she once again forgot to take note of the corridors they walked along, or the turns they took.

Looking back, Mel could see that day set the pattern for the days to come, although most days they didn't ride, spending the dawn together in bed, wrapped in a tangle of arms and legs and the warm pleasure they took from each other's bodies.

Looking back, she could see she had already been falling for the man she was to marry, although instinct told her to hide it, not only from Arun but from Jenny and Kam. Sticking to the script of how convenient it was for them to marry, for the baby, and to make it easy for her to take on this wonderful new job, setting up a paediatric surgical unit in the hospital, secure in the knowledge the baby would be well looked after and lavished with love from the family.

But when she lay in his arms on the eve of her wedding day, she allowed herself to dream, just a little, of an Arun who loved her in return. She felt the warmth of his body curled around her back, his hands tucked against the bulge that was their baby.

So he slept every night, wrapping her not only in his arms but in security, and though she told herself this was a far greater gift than love, and one that would last for ever, sometimes she ached for love as well.

Greed, that's all that is, she reminded herself as Arun stirred, his hands moving across her belly, one higher, one lower, teasing her body to life, stirring it to excitement as he awoke wanting her.

'You are one most exciting, satisfying, generous and sexy lover,' he whispered in her ear, as he pulled her closer and she felt his hard erection slide between her legs and tease its way inside her. 'Have I told you that, Mrs al'Kawali to be?'

His hands caressed her breasts.

'Have I told you how I love to touch you, to feel your body tighten as you respond to me? Have I told you your skin is softer than the softest thistledown and finer than the most expensive silk? Have I told you how I love to touch you here?'

One hand slid lower. 'And here?' A thumb and finger tweaked her nipple. 'Until you catch your breath and tighten around me and say my name in such a husky whisper I can no longer restrain myself?'

Mel bit her lip as the pressure rose inside her, sweeping her up and up in a dizzying spiral of sensation until she peaked and splintered apart and breathed his name, as he'd predicted, then felt his release and heard him sigh, his arms tightening around her as if he'd never let her go.

But a wave of melancholy swept over her as Arun eased her hair aside to press a kiss to the nape of her neck, and though she could tell herself it didn't matter, she was beginning to wonder if it did.

If loving him would prove too much for her to hide.

And, should that happen, whether him knowing would embarrass him and affect the way he held her, touched her, made love to her?

And the ache that his love-making had chased away returned…

'I'll be away tonight,' he said, all business now as he eased away from her, sitting up on the side of the bed and stretching, his toned muscles rippling beneath his satiny skin. 'I am flying out to the winter palace and won't be back until morning, but you can rest assured I will not be late for our wedding.'

He leaned across and kissed her cheek.

'And you, Madam Wife-to-be, are not to set one foot inside that hospital today. Go play with Jenny, shop, or drink coffee or do whatever women do on the day before their weddings. No work, understand?'

He tapped his finger on her nose as he gave the order, then, without waiting for a reply or a protest, rose, wrapped the white cloth he wore beneath his robes around his waist and left the bedroom, heading for his own room and the bathroom attached to it.

Mel watched him go, realising, as her melancholy deepened, that she'd never been inside that room—never been invited to see the room he considered his.

Was this room where they slept the equivalent of the women's house in the compound—a place where they could make love while his own room remained sacrosanct?

In which case, why?

She sighed.

There was only one possible reason.

Hussa!

Mel sat up, took a deep breath and tried a little positive thinking to throw off her gloom. Looking sensibly at the situation, if that *was* the case, then she, Mel, should be glad they used her bedroom, not his, for three in a bed, even when one was a ghost, was not a happy situation.

'This is a marriage of convenience,' she reminded herself, saying the words out loud to help her head remember, although it wasn't her head but her heart that needed help.

'Stupid heart,' she muttered, crossing to the bathroom and starting the shower running. 'Stupid, stupid heart.'

CHAPTER NINE

JENNY arrived as Mel was finishing her breakfast, full of plans for the day.

'I can't believe you've been here for ten days and haven't seen the city,' she announced, bubbling over not with her usual newly wed bliss but with the excitement of the proposed shopping expedition. 'Arun said we were to shop till we dropped and I was to buy you anything you wanted—a whole new wardrobe for your pregnancy and a dress for your wedding, and isn't it just the most amazing thing, the two of us falling in love with twins?'

'Marrying twins is amazing,' Mel said, 'but me marrying Arun is different—I told you that.'

Jenny smiled.

'And you can keep on telling me that,' Jenny responded, 'until you're blue in the face, but I only have to look at you when you're with Arun to realise you're in love.'

'Nonsense, that's lust, it's different,' Mel protested, because the love she held for Arun was a secret she wanted to keep hidden deep within her heart.

But to make Jen happy she shopped, allowing her friend to talk her into the most extravagant gown of golden silk for her wedding, although she stuck to practical outfits for the rest of her new wardrobe.

'I'll be working,' she reminded Jenny when they sat down for lunch in a café in the huge new shopping centre.

'Not all the time,' Jen reminded her, then she looked up and smiled as Miriam came in, having agreed to leave Tia for long enough to have lunch with the two women.

'I was telling Mel she won't be working all the time,' Jenny explained to Miriam, before turning back to Mel. 'You'll have days off to ride with

Arun and explore the country. In fact, it's surprising Arun didn't take you out to the winter palace today. It's a fascinating place.'

'I suppose because he went to talk to Hussa,' Miriam said, sounding so matter-of-fact it took a moment for Mel to process the words.

But when she did she felt the hurt—as deep as a knife thrust in her chest.

'Hussa's dead, surely?' she blurted out, dismayed by the statement and the pain.

'Of course,' Miriam agreed, still totally unperturbed. 'But her mausoleum is there. He goes to talk to her, to explain about the baby and marrying you—so it would have been rude to take you with him.'

The pain expanded, filling Mel's chest, squeezing her lungs so she could barely breathe.

Jenny was looking at her anxiously, so Mel smiled as if she'd known all along that was why she hadn't accompanied Arun, and as if it didn't matter in the least to her that her husband-to-be still talked to his dead wife. But she must have been smiling too hard, for Jenny touched her arm.

'Are you all right?'

'No,' Mel managed. 'I don't feel well. It's been coming on all morning. Must be the excitement. Do you think you could call the driver and get him to take me back to the hospital? I'll go up to the apartment and rest. You and Miriam can stay here and have lunch.'

'As if!' Jenny said, signalling to a waitress and asking her to call their driver. 'I'm coming with you.'

'No, Jen!' Mel said, looking directly at her friend so Jenny could see she meant it. 'I just need to get home and lie down for a while. I promise you I'll be all right.' She tried a smile as she added. 'Trust me, I'm a doctor.'

'Well, it doesn't seem right,' Jenny grumbled as she took Mel's arm and walked with her out to the car. 'And Arun will be furious if he hears I've let you go home on your own when you're not feeling well.'

'Arun needn't know,' Mel told her. 'Now, go back to Miriam and make sure she understands that. I'm fine, just a little woozy. It's been a kind of hectic couple of weeks.'

'It has, that,' Jenny said, kissing Mel on the cheek as the driver opened the car door for her. 'You take care and, whether you like it or not, I'm going to be calling at the apartment just as soon as Miriam and I have finished lunch, and you'd better be resting or I *will* tell Arun.'

Relief that she was finally alone flooded through Mel as the car pulled into the traffic and began the journey to the hospital. Although now she was alone, she'd have to think.

Have to work out why Miriam's words had cut into her so deeply.

She'd known all along that Arun didn't love her, so why was she upset?

Because she'd hoped he'd grow to love her— maybe had even convinced herself he was falling in love already—mistaken his natural kindness and courtesy for more than that…

The common sense part of her head was showing little mercy, but showed even less when it pursued the thoughts to their logical conclusion.

And now, it murmured to her, you know that won't happen, because no matter how he feels about you he still loves Hussa!

Oh, dear!

Back at the apartment she undressed and climbed into bed, curling herself up into a tight ball, hoping sleep might come so she didn't have to think, but sleep eluded her, which wasn't surprising, for how could she sleep when her mind kept replaying little videos of times she'd been with Arun?

Riding over the dunes, walking in the sand by moonlight, Arun soaping her back in the shower, Arun holding her as she shattered in a climax...

It was useless trying to sleep so she got up, had a shower and dressed, but what next? Arun could hardly class checking on Tia's baby as work so she left a message for Jenny with Olara and went down to the ICU, only to find Jenny and Miriam both there with Tia.

'He doesn't seem as well as he did yesterday,' Tia said, and Mel knew her instincts were probably right, although, just looking at the baby, she could see little change.

Mel checked the monitor. His pulse rate was slightly up, his blood oxygen slightly down, not enough to worry about in a healthy infant but in a baby so fragile…

She made a note for a slight change to the medication that was helping his heart and promised Tia she'd look in later. Assuring Jen she was all right now, it must just have been tiredness making her feel ill, she returned to the apartment and this time when she crawled into bed she did fall asleep, but only after she'd thought the situation through and decided what path to take.

Were her dreams bad that she frowned as she slept? Arun wondered as he stood beside the bed and watched the woman he was about to wed.

So beautiful, but did he really know her?

Not that it mattered. He told himself that repeatedly, reminding himself that no one really ever got to know another person completely. Yet it did bother him, just as her regular reminders that their marriage was a convenient arrangement bothered him.

She stirred and opened her eyes, smiling then frowning at him.

He took the fact that she smiled first as a good omen and sat down on the bed.

'You weren't coming back until tomorrow,' she said, pushing herself up on the bed until she was sitting with her back against the pillows. She frowned again. 'Did Jenny contact you?'

'No.' He answered truthfully because it was Miriam who had phoned to tell him Melissa wasn't well, and, given the frown, he guessed she'd given Jenny strict instructions to not mention her indisposition.

'Well, that's all right,' his bride-to-be announced, 'because it's good you are here. I've decided something and it's probably better I tell you today rather than tomorrow.'

This was not good, whatever it was. He knew for sure he wasn't going to like whatever was coming. And the way Melissa took a deep breath before launching into what she had to say warned him it was as bad as news could be.

'I've decided not to marry you,' she said, her

clear blue eyes steadfastly holding his. 'It won't change much. I'll live here or in the women's house and we can sleep together wherever and whenever you like and the baby will grow up in the compound with all the other kids so you will have the same paternal input into him. But we won't be married.'

The words were ringing in his head, so clear they were repeating themselves—*I've decided not to marry you*—over and over again. But they made no sense.

'You've—?'

'Decided not to marry you,' she said, as if maybe he hadn't heard the first time. 'But I can't see that it will make much difference to our lives, unless, of course, there's something really dreadful in your culture about us continuing to sleep together if we're not married, in which case that should stop, too.'

Mel ached as she said it, but she'd thought it through and decided a little pain now was better than being in pain for the rest of her life, and to marry Arun, loving him as she did, without him loving her back, would guarantee a lifetime of heartache and regret.

She watched him try to come to terms with her decision, today his thoughts not hidden from her. He was bewildered, as well he might be. So bewildered he hadn't asked the obvious question—why.

Not that she could tell him why.

Because you still love Hussa would sound lame.

She eased her legs off the bed.

'I've got to go to see the—'

The phone interrupted her. Arun lifted the receiver, and once again his face failed to hide his emotion, concern deepening to worry.

'That was Sarah Craig. The baby—'

Mel nodded, forcing everything else from her mind—all that mattered now was the baby. 'I saw him earlier,' she said. 'If he's still losing ground, I'll need to operate immediately. How quickly can you get a surgical team ready? Kam's agreed to assist. And Sarah. You'd lined up anaesthetists, perfusionists and someone who is experienced with the heart-lung machine for the op—do you think you can get them to come in tonight?'

Arun stared at her for a moment, unable to believe she'd switched from a declaration that she couldn't marry him to organising an operation in a split second.

He'd barely nodded when she continued.

'We'll need the best theatre nurses you can find—Kam will help you there—and most importantly the homograft and possibly a couple of tiny dacron ones as well in case the homograft doesn't fit. We need to move now, although we won't need the theatre team for a couple of hours. I want to be sure everything is in place before we start, and I'll want to talk to all the people who'll be in Theatre so they know what I'm doing.'

She didn't want to marry him? His mind swerved between that and business.

'I'll phone Kam then go down with you to the ICU to get the rest happening. He knows the surgical staff and can phone ahead with orders for what and who we'll need. We'll get your team if we have to fly in staff from a neighbouring country.'

Satisfied that things were moving, and with her mind now fully focussed on what lay ahead, Mel went through to the bathroom to wash before heading for the ICU.

'If he is not thriving, is it safe to operate?'

Arun was putting down the phone and asked the question as she returned to the bedroom, her hands raised as she plaited her unruly hair into a thick pigtail.

'That's the one question I'd rather you hadn't asked,' Mel said, snapping a band on her hair and turning to him with a sigh. 'I suppose it will be up to Tia. I do wish her husband was here because she shouldn't have to decide this on her own.'

'He is here, or he should be. He was due to fly in this morning. Kam arranged for him to come home as soon as we knew the baby had problems, but getting flights and connections…'

He paused, then added, 'Why are you so concerned? Why do two people need to make the decision?'

Mel sighed again.

'You must know why,' she said, cross that he was forcing her to say it. 'If the baby's health is deteriorating, it means his heart isn't coping and so we have two choices. We do nothing more than keep him comfortable until he dies, or we operate, knowing he's very young and losing the battle already, so he might die anyway.'

Arun took her hand and squeezed her fingers.

'At least that way he gets a chance,' he reminded her, but Mel refused to be comforted.

'Not that great a one,' she said. 'Think of all the variables. Will he survive a switch to a heart-lung machine? Will he even survive the anaesthetic? Will his heart muscle be patent enough for me to stitch it after the operation, will whatever homografts you have in storage be the right size? We need more than a chance, we need a miracle.'

'Miracles happen,' Arun reminded her, pulling her closer to him and holding her against his body. She hadn't mentioned no physical contact, just that she wouldn't marry him. 'Jenny and Kam

found each other and fell in love in a rebel strong-
hold, you're having the baby our country needs
as an heir. I know it seems we've had our share
of miracles, but shouldn't they come in threes?'

'I'd like to think so,' Mel said, but it was a
grudging admission, mainly because being held
in Arun's arms reminded her of all she was
turning away from with her decision to not
marry him. She pushed away.

'We've got to go,' she said, and left the room.

The little boy was struggling, his lips much bluer
than they had been when Mel had seen him only
hours earlier, his oxygen stats on their own low
enough to be a concern. Mel examined him, an
anxious Sarah hovering by her side.

'It happened so suddenly I thought at first the
monitors must be playing up,' the anxious young
doctor said.

'It can happen quickly,' Mel assured her.
'Don't blame yourself. Where's Tia?'

'In the visitors' room across the hall,' Sarah responded, nodding towards the small room

families used as a refuge. 'Dr al'Kawali went in there to talk to her.'

Mel finished her examination, then made her way to the next room.

Tia sat on the couch with a young man in jeans and a polo shirt, looking so anxious he had to be the baby's father. Arun squatted in front of the pair, his hands holding a hand of each of them.

'I have told them the two options,' he said to Mel as she entered the room.

Mel felt relief, then wondered how much time the young parents would need to discuss these unhappy options.

'We want to go ahead with the operation,' Tia said, looking directly at Mel. 'That was what I had already decided, and when my husband was asked, he said the same. The baby deserves to have the chance of life and without the operation that is taken from him.'

'You understand he still might not live,' Mel pressed, because she had to hear for herself that they had considered that.

Both heads nodded, and the young man reached out to clasp his wife's hands.

'OK, we go ahead,' Mel told them. 'I'm going to take him now to Radiology for some scans while Arun collects the team of people we'll need for the operation and Kam organises the theatre and makes sure we have everything we need on hand.'

She looked at the two young people, so patently lost in their concern and grief, and stretched out her hands to them.

'It's going to be a long, hard wait for you two. Why don't you go somewhere private—maybe out to the compound—so you can comfort each other and perhaps even think of other things while the operation is going on?'

Tia looked at Mel and managed a weak smile.

'Private at the compound? I don't think so. No, we'll stay here in my room. We'll sit and talk and pray and know you're doing the best you can for our baby.'

She took her husband's hand and led him away. Arun turned to watch them go, a small, sad smile on his face.

'So my baby sister has grown up,' he said quietly, and Mel felt the weight of what she was about to undertake press down on her. So many people wanting this baby to live—so many people's happiness dependent on this operation...

She straightened up and took a deep breath. She could do this!

She went back to the baby's room

'Come on, kid,' she said to the little mite in the crib. 'Let's get you sorted.'

To Arun the most amazing thing was the noise in the room. He'd imagined operating theatres as places of deep quietness, but here, as he stood beside Kam, second assistant and general dogsbody, it was the noise that struck him.

He tried to think back to his student days when he'd done stints in Theatre, but although he remembered music playing in the background, and surgeons telling stupid jokes as they worked, he didn't remember the buzz of the Bovie as small blood vessels were sealed off or the blip of the heart monitor and the puffing noise of the ventilator.

He looked at the tiny baby on the table, his eyes taped closed, a ventilation tube in his trachea, a tube feeding into the radial artery at his wrist, a central line in the jugular vein in his neck and a fourth line, just in case, in his foot. The anaesthetist was organising the necessary mix of gases into the stressed lungs and the drugs that were needed in the blood. Heparin, Arun knew, to thin the blood so it wouldn't clog up the heart-lung machine when the little one went on bypass. The anaesthetist had everything on hand, blood, saline, drugs, ready for any emergency. The perfusionist was taking blood all the time, checking the balance, while the monitor showed everyone in the room the baby's blood pressure, heart rate, oxygen saturation and temperature.

Melissa had used shears to cut the small chest open, and while he held it open with retractors Kam had fitted brackets to the sides of the sternum and turned a handle—more noise—to give Melissa a good opening to work in.

The heart-lung machine was ready, the baby's temperature was being reduced and they were approaching the moment when he would be connected to the machine.

'I'm cutting these small pieces of pericardium to use as a patch for the ventricular septum,' Melissa explained, using a stitch to secure two small squares of the pericardial tissue to an intercostal muscle. 'By stitching it there I'm not frantically looking for it when I need it. Now I use a stitch to keep the pericardium out of the way so we can get to the heart cleanly.'

Arun knew she was explaining this for the benefit of Sarah, who was in Theatre with them, but he couldn't help feeling proud that she was making the effort to explain while ninety-nine per cent of her mind must be concentrated on the difficult task.

'Now we put a cannula into the aorta, and it will send blood from the machine around the body while this cannula goes into the right atrium and we'll be sucking blood through it into the machine. Heart rate?'

'One-thirty,' someone answered.

'Temp?'

'Thirty.'

Arun shivered, thinking how cold the deep hypothermia must be, but it slowed the heart rate and made it easier to transfer the baby to the machine.

'Now we need to check the pulmonary artery. We come back from where it divides to right and left arteries to where it merges with the aorta—that's where we cut and put in the grafted artery. We'll fix that to the right ventricle…'

He was following it all, mainly because Melissa had called them all together earlier and drawn diagrams on a whiteboard, taking everyone who'd be involved through every stage of the operation. But how could she be so calm, operating on a baby—stitching together blood vessels so small one misplaced stitch could close them completely?

Yet she worked with a concentration that excluded all outside thoughts, quietly telling Kam what needed to be done, giving orders to the theatre staff to tie this, Bovie that, suction here, check the screen. And as he watched, and helped, he felt a sense of pride. This was *his* woman, doing this—*his* woman producing the miracle the baby needed.

Or was she?

She'd said she wouldn't marry him.

Why now?

What had happened to make her change her mind?

And why was it so hard to accept?

Painfully hard.

'OK, now we go. Pavulon to paralyse the heart muscle then we're going onto the machine— you all know what you need to do.'

Arun forgot everything but the baby on the table, and even the theatre noises seemed to abate as Melissa cut and stitched, fixing up the malformation that something as simple as a virus in Tia's early pregnancy might have caused.

He stood beside Kam, suctioning, passing instruments, tossing debris away, totally concentrated on the baby now, barely breathing, although he didn't realise that until Melissa said, 'OK, coming off bypass now,' and he had to take a gulp of air.

'This is the moment,' Kam whispered to him as Melissa reconnected the baby's vein and artery then massaged the heart to get it beating. Drugs were flowing into him to stimulate the heart, and those gathered in the room held their collective breaths and waited for the heart muscles to contract and lift the floppy, patched and stitched heart back to a working organ.

'There,' someone said, and they were right. The little heart was beating valiantly. Arun looked across at Melissa and behind the goggles she was wearing he saw the brightness of tears in her eyes. She must have sensed his regard for she looked at him and shook her head.

'That's the easy part,' she said lightly, although he could hear exhaustion in her voice and knew how much it had taken out of her. 'Now we have to put him back together again, then get him through the after-effects of the terrible trauma we've caused him. First off, Kam, could you check for bleeding on any of the joins we've made? And I want oxygen stats, BP and heart rate. No point sewing him up if there's still a problem somewhere.'

The results must have pleased her for within

minutes she bent her head again, working swiftly and surely, putting, as she'd said, the little baby back together again.

'I'll stay with the anaesthetist and the baby,' Kam said to Arun when Melissa finally stepped back from the operating table. 'You take Melissa back to the apartment. She'll be exhausted—it's mental strain as much as the physical effort of concentration. Tell her I'll call if there's any change.'

Arun moved away—the theatre was noisy again, instruments clanging together, people talking, most in awed tones, as they cleared away the debris of a long operation. Melissa was at the far side of the room, stripping off her gloves, the fourth set she'd worn during the operation.

'Come, there's a room here where you can change in privacy, then I'll take you home and get some food and drink into you—you must be totally depleted.'

She had slid the goggles she'd been wearing to the top of her head, and now pulled them off.

'Home?' she echoed, a tired smile on her face.

'The apartment, you know I meant that—no

talk, hidden agenda, not after what you've just done for us.'

She shook her head.

'Not for you, but for the baby. Not even for Tia and her husband, just for the baby.'

She pressed her hand against her stomach, and he wondered how often she worried whether the child she carried was OK. Working with babies with congenital conditions, she couldn't help but wonder...

'So, where's this private space?'

Her apron and outer gown had joined her mask, gloves and goggles in the bin and she stood there in the pale green scrub suit, looking so spent he wanted to lift her into his arms and carry her back to the apartment.

'This way. Your clothes are there, but if you don't want to change, you can come up to the apartment as you are and shower there.'

'I'll do that—just get out of the boots and into my sandals. Thanks.'

But as she was about to leave the theatre complex she turned back.

'The baby?'

'Kam will stay with him. He'll contact you immediately if there's any change or any cause for concern.'

She nodded and Arun realised just how tired she must be to not argue that he too should stay, or even she herself.

Mel let him take charge, leading her out of the warren of rooms around the theatre then up to the apartment, where with gentle hands he stripped off her clothes and helped her step into the shower, already running at a beautiful temperature, the water jets spraying from the wall just what she needed for her aching back.

Eventually, certain her skin had shrivelled to crêpe, she left the shower, to find Arun waiting once again, wrapping her in a big warm towel, then leading her to the bedroom where he sat her on the bed while he towel-dried her hair.

'Now, you're to eat—doctor's orders,' he said, and Mel looked around, saw daylight at the window and frowned.

'It's morning?'

Arun nodded.

'We went down to the baby's room at six last night and you've been working ever since,' he said. 'You were in Theatre five hours.'

'It didn't seem that long,' Mel managed, but as she spoke she felt a wave of tiredness bear down on her, all but engulfing her.

She sipped some tea and ate two pancakes, then shook her head.

'No more. I really, really need to sleep.'

But as she set her cup down she thought of the baby and looked up at Arun.

'You *will* wake me up if I'm needed?' she demanded. 'No nonsense about letting the poor little woman sleep?'

He smiled and in spite of her tiredness and her determination to stop loving him, her heart beat faster.

'Poor little woman indeed,' he teased. 'Woe betide any man who dared to use that description for you.'

Then he bent and kissed her on the lips.

'I will wake you up,' he promised. 'You can be sure of that, so sleep at peace, my beautiful one.'

She lay back on the pillows and he drew the sheet over her naked body, then touched her gently on the cheek and left the room.

'My beautiful one?' Mel murmured to herself, savouring the words, then she remembered back before the operation.

Remembered telling him they wouldn't marry…

Remembered he hadn't asked why…

She turned on her side, tucked her hands beneath her head and sighed, though for what she wasn't quite sure, and she was too darned tired to think about it now.

'His name is Shiar.'

Tia rose from beside the crib in the ICU room to greet Mel with this news as Mel, refreshed, fed and anxious to see her patient, entered at about midday.

'Oh, I'm so glad you've named him,' Mel told her, giving the young woman a quick hug.

'And you didn't meet Sharif, my husband— not properly,' Tia added, introducing Mel formally to the young man who bowed over her hand and rushed into a welter of thanks for all she had done for the baby.

'It is nothing,' she said, resting her hand on the sleeve of the white gown he now wore. 'And the little one, Shiar, is still far from well. We must wait and see.'

Both parents nodded, but Mel could read the hope in their shining eyes and prayed it would not be misplaced.

She checked Shiar, who was to be kept sedated for at least twenty-four hours, then said goodbye to the pair, but once outside the baby's room she leaned against the wall, uncertain what to do next.

It was to be her wedding day so the women who were still trickling into the A and E department with sick children had been told she wouldn't be available, although, having assured Arun she intended to keep working, she did have appointments lined up for the following day.

But today?

Perhaps she could ride. She'd go out to the compound—

'I was looking for you.'

Arun had pushed through the doors into the ICU without her noticing.

'Come!' he said, and took her hand. 'I want to take you somewhere.'

She tried to tug her hand away but his grip was too strong.

'I'm not going with you to get married,' she told him, and he smiled the kind of knowing smile that *always* made her heart flutter. Only today it made her angry as well and she tugged again at her trapped hand.

'Did I mention marriage?' he teased, releasing her hand but slipping his arm through hers so she would have to make a scene to escape his touch.

They reached the bank of lifts and to Mel's surprise he pushed the 'up' button rather than the 'down' one.

'We're going up? Are your rooms up? No, they're on the same floor as the ICU, aren't they? Why are we going up?'

'You'll see,' he said.

And Mel did, for the doors of the lift opened onto a flat roof and there, not forty feet in front of them, was a small green helicopter.

'I thought I'd show you my kingdom,' he said, leading her towards it. 'So you can see what you're missing out on by not marrying me.'

Mel frowned at him. Surely he couldn't think she would have been marrying him for riches or property or to be the sheikhess—no, that was wrong, Jenny was a sheikha. But her annoyance was more than outweighed by excitement that she would be seeing more of this beautiful desert country. With Arun…

He helped her into the helicopter then walked around and climbed in on the other side, taking the controls himself.

'There are parts of the land where you can't fly helicopters—out near the mountains where Jenny was, for instance—but most of the country is accessible this way and flying takes many hours off a journey.'

His long slender fingers worked easily at the

controls and the little machine lifted into the air and took off, circling the city first, Arun pointing out the port where ships from all over the world docked to take on oil, and the swathes of green contrasting with the red-brown desert sands—golf courses and resorts—playgrounds of the wealthy. Then the city disappeared and beneath them lay the desert, dotted here and there with encampments of black tents or clusters of palms that indicated oases.

'This is the long wadi—there are oases all along it,' Arun explained as they banked over a small village, stone and earth brick houses clustered by the green patch of vegetation. 'And here we are—see below—the winter palace.'

The winter palace?

Where Hussa was buried?

Mel felt her chest grow tight and her breathing become shallow and irregular. Why was he bringing her here?

She turned towards him, wanting to ask, not about Hussa but about the reason for the visit, but he was concentrating on putting the little aircraft down on the ground, onto a white circle painted on a concrete pad just outside the walls of the rambling, red stone building he'd called the winter palace.

CHAPTER TEN

HE TURNED the engine off and climbed out, ducking beneath the slowing rotor blades to come around and open the door on her side.

'Come,' he said once more, the word peremptory but not an order. He took her hand to help her alight then led her towards the long shallow steps that rose towards the entrance of the huge, many-turreted building.

'In the old days, when this was first built, it was a fort as well as a home, so instead of many buildings, as we have in the city compound, all the functions are in one main palace, broken up into many...I suppose you would say apartments—for different families and different uses.'

Mel looked around. The red stone, much of it

ornately carved, was old enough to be crumbling in places, but she could see the design of an ancient fort in it, for the windows were narrow slits, many of them inset with carved stonework. Huge wooden doors were folded back and they walked beneath an arch and into a courtyard, not landscaped, as the city courtyard was, but cobbled.

Around the courtyard was a cloister, and Mel glimpsed, here and there, robed figures flitting through the shadows.

'It was here the men prepared their mounts and armed themselves for raids,' Arun said. 'It was built for practicality, not beauty, but walk carefully—the cobbles are old and very rough in parts.'

He took her arm, drawing her across and to the left where they passed into the shadow of the cloister and shed their sandals before entering the building. Once inside she had to gasp for instead of the red stone all was cool white marble—the floor, the pillars, the walls, all the same white-grey, streaked here and there with black, and inlaid in the arches and above the windows with what looked like precious gems.

'You cannot show your wealth to the enemy,' Arun explained, leading from room to room, pointing out the tapestries and telling her the history of his family that was depicted in them, showing her the great hall where he and Kam would still hold audiences for their people, listening to grievances, trying to right wrongs.

Then up a winding staircase, into one of the turrets.

'We played here as children, Kam and I, although we were forbidden to do so,' he said, and she could imagine the twins racing each other up the stairs.

'Or perhaps because you were forbidden,' Mel said, knowing the lure of the forbidden to a child. 'But is the whole place deserted now?' she asked, thinking of the waste that all the rooms should be empty.

'Far from it,' he said, leading her out onto a small balcony that ran around the top of the turret. 'Look.'

He pointed down and she saw that he'd landed on the shortest side of the huge building and led her into only one part of it. Below them was another courtyard, thick with palms and fruit trees, where men raked paths, and women walked, and children played.

'When my father was alive, he wanted all the family to live here permanently and used whatever pressure he could, financial and emotional, to keep them here. I imagine it was part rebellion against his strictures that when he died most of them immediately moved to the city. But a couple of my sisters, some aunts and a few unrelated dependants still live out here all year round. Some prefer the old to the new.'

'It's very beautiful,' Mel said, seeing the stunted date palms from the top and yellow lemons bright against the glossy leaves of their trees.

'This part I have been showing you was my father's domain,' Arun continued. 'Kam hates it still, but it has always had a special place in my heart, in spite of the unhappiness the old man caused us. Knowing this, Kam has insisted it be mine and after me it will be my child's, because this is his or her history and heritage. I thought, in seeing it, you might understand why marriage is important to me.'

Mel could, but the word 'marriage' reminded Mel of Miriam's words in the shopping centre.

'You came here yesterday?' Mel began, unsure what to say next.

Arun looked puzzled for a moment, then frowned.

'Miriam told you? Yes, I did.'

He hesitated and Mel felt the chill of Hussa's ghost floating between them.

Then Arun took her hand and held it gently, as if it was something very precious.

'My first wife, Hussa, is buried here. I came to see her, Mel, to tell her all about you and about the happiness you've brought me, and as I sat there, I realised she would want me to be happy. It was an ending, Mel, so I could move on. So I could marry you—or so I thought.'

He was studying her face and although she could feel happiness singing in her blood, uncertainty held her mute.

Fortunately, Arun still retained the power of words. In a voice husky with an emotion she dared not guess at he said, 'But you should know, Melissa, that I won't force you to marry me any more…'

He paused and looked out over the buildings and beyond them to the desert, baking under the afternoon sun.

Then he turned and took her hands and looked at her.

'Any more,' he continued, 'than I can force you to love me.'

Mel frowned at him, the words not computing into anything intelligible in her head.

'Force me to love you?' she repeated. 'Why would you say that?'

A self-deprecating little smile pressed a line into his left cheek.

'Because love has been off limits? Because of your insistence that our marriage is a practical arrangement? Because it's so damn difficult for me to believe what I feel, let alone make a fool of myself by telling you?'

He turned away as if looking at her caused him pain, but Mel was catching up.

'Arun?'

He swung back to look at her, strain around his mouth now and uncertainty in his eyes.

'Make a fool of yourself,' she begged, smiling at him as she said it. 'Tell me.'

He sighed, then shook his head, the in-control sheikh suddenly lost.

'I love you,' he managed, then added, 'There, it's said!'

And sighed again.

'That's all?' Mel teased, so happy she wanted to leap into the air and shout her joy to the world but holding it all under control because she wasn't finished with this man yet.

'Isn't it enough?' he grumbled, as if sure he'd made a total idiot of himself.

'Of course it's not,' Mel told him. 'Now you have to kiss me and tell me why you love me and whisper sweet nothings in my ear.'

'Sweet nothings?' he repeated, suspicion

dawning in his eyes. 'You're happy about this? You're not annoyed?'

Mel smiled at him and put her arms around him, drawing close to his body.

'Why would I be annoyed when you've just made me the happiest woman in the world?' she murmured. 'When you've just told me the love I have for you is returned. When—'

'Love is returned? You love me, too?'

He pushed away so he could look into her face.

'If you love me, why did you say you wouldn't marry me?' he demanded, and Mel drew him close again, embarrassed by the intensity of her feelings and not wanting him looking at her as she confessed.

'I thought you didn't love me—couldn't see why you would—especially when you'd so loved Hussa. Then I thought loving you without you loving me back would be easier if we weren't married than if we were, so...'

Arun put his hands on her shoulders and eased her away, his face stern now.

'Let us back up a bit here,' he said, his voice

stern as well. 'I know we never talked of love, but surely you must have had some inkling of how I felt? And as for Hussa, yes, Melissa, I did love her, but she is gone and you have come to fill all the empty places in my heart. You must understand that or you will make yourself miserable. It is you I love—my brave, strong, independent, argumentative and beautiful Melissa. You I love now and will love for ever.'

And finally he kissed her, so sweetly, so tenderly Mel wondered if her heart might burst apart with the love it held, although she knew full well hearts were very tough structures and hers would probably handle the strain.

EPILOGUE

Two women robed in blue sat on easy chairs beneath the lemon trees in the courtyard, warmed by the sun reflecting off the red stone building.

'Bliss?' Mel said, turning to pick up the baby girl who grizzled quietly in a woven basket by her side.

'Bliss!' Jenny echoed, lying back, her hands linked around her bulging stomach. 'Although it would be nicer if the men were here.'

'Your wish is their command, I'd say,' Mel said, turning her head the better to hear the rattling noise of the approaching helicopter.

It flew over them like a shiny green dragonfly, swooping low enough to make Mel shake her fist at the pilot.

'He knows not to do that in case it wakes the baby,' she told her friend.

'The baby's already awake,' Jenny reminded her, nodding to the chubby infant sucking greedily on Melissa's breast.

'But she might not have been,' Mel complained, although her heart wasn't in it. Her heart, in fact, was dancing with excitement, although Arun had only been gone a couple of days—down to the city to the opening of the now completed renovations of the old hospital.

'So, the lazy women of the harem are taking their ease.'

It was Kam who spoke as the two brothers entered the courtyard, so alike yet easily identifiable to their wives.

'It's not exactly ease when I'm having Braxton-Hicks's contractions all the time,' Jen told him, though she rose to go towards him, greeting him with a kiss and turning in his arms so they could walk together. 'To think of all I went through to have this baby—operation after operation—and now it's doing this to me.'

'Ah, but it will all be worth it when you hold him in your arms,' Mel said. 'I think I was as excited as you were when you finally fell pregnant and then to learn it was a boy. Zaheer may be developing quickly but I'm not sure they'd be ready for a female ruler.'

'Or that my sweet little Nooria would want the job,' Arun said, reaching Mel's side and kneeling by her, his eyes feasting on his daughter.

'Sweet *little* Nooria?' Mel responded. 'This child is going to be the size of an oil drum, the way she eats.'

'She is beautiful,' Arun whispered, running his hand over the downy head. 'As is her mother.'

He reached up to touch Mel's lips with his fingers.

'You are well?'

Mel nodded, the emotion she felt tightening her chest too much for her to be able to speak.

How could it be that love could grow so much? That what she had felt for Arun when they'd married, a couple of days later than they'd planned, could be but a shadow of the love that had grown between them in the year that had followed?

'Is all prepared for the party?' Arun asked, and Mel found her voice.

'That's why we had to rest—we haven't stopped. That sister of yours is a slave-driver.'

She eased the baby off her breast and Arun helped her stand, then he slipped his arm around her and the five of them made their way into the grand hall, not for an audience today but to celebrate the first birthday of a very special, and very healthy, little boy.

Shiar.

But as Kam and Jenny walked under the arch into the cloister, Mel paused, turning to look back at the courtyard, seeing the greens of the trees deepen as the sun sank lower in the sky then the flush of colour above the palace walls as the magical evening light show began.

Arun turned with her.

'You are happy, my love?' he asked quietly.

She moved closer to his side and rested her head on his shoulder.

'Happier than I ever thought a woman could be, Arun. And you?'

His arm tightened around her shoulder and he bent awkwardly around Nooria to kiss Mel on the lips.

'How could I not be when you have given me so great a gift—when you have given me your love?'

MEDICAL™

―――――――ᐯ― *Large Print* ―――ᐯ―

Titles for the next six months…

December

SINGLE DAD SEEKS A WIFE	Melanie Milburne
HER FOUR-YEAR BABY SECRET	Alison Roberts
COUNTRY DOCTOR, SPRING BRIDE	Abigail Gordon
MARRYING THE RUNAWAY BRIDE	Jennifer Taylor
THE MIDWIFE'S BABY	Fiona McArthur
THE FATHERHOOD MIRACLE	Margaret Barker

January

VIRGIN MIDWIFE, PLAYBOY DOCTOR	Margaret McDonagh
THE REBEL DOCTOR'S BRIDE	Sarah Morgan
THE SURGEON'S SECRET BABY WISH	Laura Iding
PROPOSING TO THE CHILDREN'S DOCTOR	Joanna Neil
EMERGENCY: WIFE NEEDED	Emily Forbes
ITALIAN DOCTOR, FULL-TIME FATHER	Dianne Drake

February

THEIR MIRACLE BABY	Caroline Anderson
THE CHILDREN'S DOCTOR AND THE SINGLE MUM	Lilian Darcy
THE SPANISH DOCTOR'S LOVE-CHILD	Kate Hardy
PREGNANT NURSE, NEW-FOUND FAMILY	Lynne Marshall
HER VERY SPECIAL BOSS	Anne Fraser
THE GP'S MARRIAGE WISH	Judy Campbell

MILLS & BOON®

Pure reading pleasure™

1108 LP 2P P1 Medical

MEDICAL™

—∿— *Large Print* —∿—

March

SHEIKH SURGEON CLAIMS HIS BRIDE Josie Metcalfe
A PROPOSAL WORTH WAITING FOR   Lilian Darcy
A DOCTOR, A NURSE: A LITTLE MIRACLE Carol Marinelli
TOP-NOTCH SURGEON, PREGNANT NURSE Amy Andrews
A MOTHER FOR HIS SON   Gill Sanderson
THE PLAYBOY DOCTOR'S MARRIAGE   Fiona Lowe
PROPOSAL

April

A BABY FOR EVE   Maggie Kingsley
MARRYING THE MILLIONAIRE DOCTOR Alison Roberts
HIS VERY SPECIAL BRIDE   Joanna Neil
CITY SURGEON, OUTBACK BRIDE   Lucy Clark
A BOSS BEYOND COMPARE   Dianne Drake
THE EMERGENCY DOCTOR'S   Molly Evans
CHOSEN WIFE

May

DR DEVEREUX'S PROPOSAL   Margaret McDonagh
CHILDREN'S DOCTOR,   Meredith Webber
MEANT-TO-BE WIFE
ITALIAN DOCTOR, SLEIGH-BELL BRIDE Sarah Morgan
CHRISTMAS AT WILLOWMERE   Abigail Gordon
DR ROMANO'S CHRISTMAS BABY   Amy Andrews
THE DESERT SURGEON'S SECRET SON   Olivia Gates

MILLS & BOON®
Pure reading pleasure™   1108 LP 2P P2 Medical